"I knew there was a flesh-and-blood woman under the lady," Reeve drawled.

China's knees weakened as his eyes traveled over her with the intimate languor a man might use to view a life-size nude. The deep V-neck of her dress flattered every curve of her statuesque figure, and the unusual shade of stormy-blue silk coaxed her eyes to luminous gray-blue. Reeve leaned forward, taking a breath of her perfume, inhaling its fragrant promise.

"Mmmm, nice," he murmured.

Sensations swamped China, and she moved back a step, out of the danger zone. "Isn't it against the law to park on the sidewalk?"

"I'm not sure." He grinned. "I specialize in corporate law."

They turned to leave the apartment, Reeve's muscled body trapping China in a hallway corner.

"Advantage, Laughlin," he said quietly. Her gaze jumped to his face. Flames heated his eyes, and China narrowed hers instinctively.

"You're confusing your tennis with your chess," China replied. She had intended the words to be cool and impassive; instead, her voice was too husky, too breathless.

"I don't care what the name of the game is . . . so long as we play. . . ."

WHAT ARE *LOVESWEPT* ROMANCES?

They are stories of true romance and touching emotion. We believe those two very important ingredients are constants in our highly sensual and very believable stories in the *LOVESWEPT* line. Our goal is to give you, the reader, stories of consistently high quality that may sometimes make you laugh, sometimes make you cry, but are always fresh and creative and contain many delightful surprises within their pages.

Most romance fans read an enormous number of books. Those they truly love, they keep. Others may be traded with friends and soon forgotten. We hope that each *LOVESWEPT* romance will be a treasure—a "keeper." We will always try to publish

*LOVE STORIES YOU'LL NEVER FORGET
BY AUTHORS YOU'LL ALWAYS REMEMBER*

The Editors

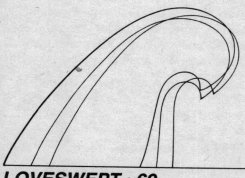

LOVESWEPT · 69

Marianne Shock
Queen's Defense

BANTAM BOOKS
TORONTO · NEW YORK · LONDON · SYDNEY · AUCKLAND

QUEEN'S DEFENSE
A Bantam Book / November 1984

LOVESWEPT and the wave device are trademarks
of Bantam Books, Inc.

ISBN 0-553-21677-5

Published simultaneously in the United States and Canada

PRINTED IN THE UNITED STATES OF AMERICA

O   0 9 8 7 6 5 4 3 2 1

"This book is dedicated to my sister, Jody, for her assistance; for never being too busy or too tired—for always believing—with much love."

One

Contracts. How she hated them! China studied the sheaf of papers spread out on her desk, curling back the upper right-hand corner of one page as she read the small print for the fourth time. Her loose black hair spilled over one shoulder, and she flipped it out of her way, sighing with frustration. She loathed going over her clients' contracts as fiercely as she loved being a talent agent.

The interruption of her telephone intercom was welcomed with a smile. China slipped off her pearl earring and reached for the phone. "Yes, Marce."

"Line two, China . . . an attorney from Hoffer, Kole."

"Hoffer, Kole?" What in the world did New York City's most prestigious law firm want with China or the Payne Agency?

"Something about your mother," Marce warned.

China promptly drew her finger back from the flashing line-two button. Damn! What now? Her hand curled into a fist as she realized it could only mean another ridiculous lawsuit. Let's see: last time her mother had tried to sue a beauty salon for mixing the hair dye improperly, causing temporary baldness—it wasn't even her mother's salon or her mother's hair . . . only a case she had read about in the paper. The clear plastic button on the phone flickered on and off while China hesitated. Along with prestigious, Hoffer, Kole was conservative—far too conservative to be party to one of her mother's preposterous antic lawsuits.

Oh, Lord, she prayed silently as she put her finger to the glowing button. Whatever it is, keep it out of the papers this time.

She took a deep breath, gathering courage, and tapped into line two. "China Payne here."

"Reeve Laughlin," a gritty, deep-timbered voice responded. A prickle of foreboding rose up in China at the man's name. "Do I have the right China Payne?" he asked. "Your mother's name is Clare?"

Damn, this wasn't a lawsuit. It was worse!

"Hello?" Reeve Laughlin barked. "You there?"

"You have the right China Payne," she acknowledged. "You have also wasted your time. We have nothing to talk about."

"You know who I am, then?"

Her knuckles grew white as her grip on the phone tightened and the grip on her composure started to slip. "I assume you are related to my stepfather, Martin Laughlin."

"I'm his son."

Son! Brother or cousin, China had expected. But son? Another stepbrother?

"I still have nothing to say to you," China said with finality.

"Don't hang up," he ordered. Her feathery black lashes shot up as she stared at the receiver. She had been about to do just that! "I can be in your office in a matter of minutes. And that's exactly where you'll find me if you hang up the phone," the man threatened.

"Make it fast, Mr. Laughlin," China conceded. "I'm very busy."

"*You're* busy? Ms. Payne, I haven't done a decent day's work for nearly a week. If your mother isn't pestering my office by phone, she's making appointments she doesn't keep. She's broken another one today and informed my secretary that I'm to be at her apartment at two o'clock. She ended with the ominous warning that my father's life hangs in the balance."

"I suggest you be there then, Mr. Laughlin."

"It's not that simple. When I phoned for the address, someone named Elly—"

"Milly," China corrected.

"What?"

"The housekeeper. Her name is Milly."

"Fine, Milly." He curtly bit each word off. "This Milly won't put your mother on the phone. 'Clare is indisposed,' she says. Nor will she let me in at two o'clock unless you—"

"I'll call her."

"I suggested that, but Tilly—"

"Milly."

"But *that woman* was very definite: No one gets in that apartment without China Payne. I'll be honest with you, Ms. Payne. Until your mother called me last Monday, I had no idea my father had remarried, and frankly I didn't much care. But if his life is in danger, if he's ill or something, I want to know about it. So like it or not, you're going to get me into that apartment. I'll pick you up at one-thirty."

Reeve Laughlin was proving himself to be his father's son all right, China told herself. Selfish and arrogant. Given the chance, China suspected he would prove himself to be as unprincipled as Martin. "Again you've wasted your time."

"We can do this the easy way, Ms. Payne, in which case you'll come with me when I arrive. Or we can do this the hard way, and you'll *still* come with me. I'm a big man physically."

Now it was her turn to sense his intentions. "Don't hang up!" A click and a dial tone followed her demand.

She dropped the receiver to its cradle. Shoving her swivel chair around one hundred eighty degrees, she stared out the plate-glass window at her view of New York. The sun-starved October morning made a bleak, gray sculpture of the city, which didn't do much for her mood. She propped her feet on the window casing and glanced down the length of her legs stretched out in front of her. She was five feet ten barefoot; he would have to be a *very* big man.

She gnawed at her full bottom lip, and her gray eyes grew large and round as she stared off in the distance. What the hell was Clare up to? Four months ago her mother had married Martin Laughlin; two weeks ago Martin had walked out. And now, out of the blue, a son suddenly shows up. Was Martin's life really in danger? Had Clare even had contact with him?

There was a double-time rap on her door and Marce entered. "Done with that?" she asked. China glanced over her shoulder to see the petite brunette's nod at the contract.

"Send it down to legal," China said. "Ask for each clause to be summarized in layman's language, particularly the fifth and eighth. Then get the studio that sent it to us on the phone and find out why they've altered a standard contract to read like a major corporate merger."

Marce departed with the sticky contract in hand. The Payne Agency, only three years old, was just now able to support an adequate staff of secretaries, talent scouts, and coordinators. An in-house attorney was a luxury China could not afford. "Legal" referred to a budding law firm in the same building, eager for the business and qualified to solve *that* problem.

Which brought her face-to-face with the more immediate matter of Reeve Laughlin. Should she call him back? Was there any point? He hadn't sounded like a man who was agreeable to compromise or negotiation.

With only a faint glimmer of hope China dialed her mother's number. Hope died when the answering service picked up. Thirty years as Clare's daughter had left China with enough experiences in her mother's unpredictable ways to begin worrying.

Clare had been the pampered only child of Lester Howard, one of Hollywood's original film producers. Lester had lived a luxuriously flamboyant life in California. His parties had drawn the wealthy, the decadent . . . and the press. While he lived, he cultivated in Clare a taste for outrageous living, and when he died, he left her enough of his vastly diminished fortune to support her self-indulgence for a good many years to come.

To China, his only grandchild at the time of his death, he had left a generous sum of money. She had been born with his unerring ability to understand, pacify, and promote the volatile and unsteady ego of the actor. After her divorce three years ago China had spent her inheritance opening her agency. It had taken every dollar in the bank and every minute of her life to get this far. The Payne Agency was her career, her home, her baby. She had no time or desire for anything else.

Now, glancing around her teal-blue and alabaster office, she had the uneasy feeling that something, or someone, had just invaded her preciously private domain. And it wasn't Clare! There had been other phone calls about her, and China had accepted the role-reversal of daughter as guardian and mother as ward.

No, it was Reeve Laughlin who made her want to jump up and lock all the doors. For no other reason, China admitted, than that he was her stepbrother, and a lawyer. Countless lawyers were now top-drawer attorneys because they had represented Clare in some lunacy, milking the story for every inch of publicity—good, bad, or indifferent—as long as it kept their names in front of the public. Then China's own lawyer had pulled the same grandstand stunt when she had divorced Paul Doran, her last stepbrother.

Reeve Laughlin was an unsettling combination of two sorts that had caused China heartache. He stood little chance of anything more than a civil welcome. If that, China thought.

At one-twenty Marce again buzzed her employer. Curled up on China's sofa was Amanda Temple, her pale soft shape blending with the eggshell-colored upholstery. "Yes, Marce," China said with a sigh into the phone.

"Mr. Laughlin to see you," came the frosty reply.

"He's early, tell him to wait."

"Ah . . . China?" Marce's voice dropped to a whisper. From the hushed tone China knew the girl was hunched away from the visitor and hiding the mouthpiece behind a cupped hand. "Have you ever met this guy? I mean, face-to-face?"

China's irritation with the Laughlin family was being pushed to aggravation. "What are you trying to say, Marce?"

"I thought not! He sort of reminds me of a Siberian tiger. Magnificent to look at, but you don't exactly go ordering it around."

"I don't care if he's a three-ton dinosaur," China

snapped. "Tell him he's early. His time, for which he will receive a bill, begins at one-thirty. Period."

"You really want me to say *that*?"

"Precisely that!" China slammed the phone down and turned to Mandy. With a nod of her head she urged the girl to go on with the scene she was rehearsing.

Nine and a half minutes later a man barged into her office.

His eyes fell on a willowy girl with pale blue eyes and a mantle of silver-white hair. The glitter of tears streaked her small-featured face, and she seemed on the verge of collapse. Reeve tried to connect the throaty voice on the phone to this little thing portraying a distraught figure. Impossible! The only thing predictable about her at all was that she resembled a delicate china figurine.

"You are intruding, Mr. Laughlin," the familiar, husky voice said. Only it didn't come from the wispy girl nestled on the sofa. Reeve swung around to see another woman, this one standing behind, and holding on to, a wide desk. His eyes automatically went to the spot he had accustomed his stare for women, and had to go up six inches from a button on her apricot-colored silk blouse.

China was furious. For a professional he was surprisingly unprofessional. Her fists gripped the desk tighter as she met the electric blue eyes of the man who had just stormed into her office. He was absolutely devastating. Too rugged and tough to be called handsome. His was that daring, adventurous look agents scoured their files to find.

"It is one-thirty," he said, tapping his finger to his watch. Then his sapphire eyes ran down the length of her body as far as the desk top. China thought she saw his pupils dilate.

"Reconsidering your threat to throw me over your

shoulder and carry me out of here, Mr. Laughlin? It could be more difficult than you expected."

"Not too," he drawled. Tall enough for China to look up to, he had a wide-shouldered, lean-hipped build, and his navy-blue suit fit every inch of it to perfection. Yet something wasn't quite right. His hair? As black as her own, his unruly mane had been tamed with a layer cut and styled to cling to his shirt collar. That was it! It was too long for a lawyer, especially one from the conservative firm of Hoffer, Kole.

"Well," he growled. "Do we do this easy? Or hard?"

China turned to Amanda, uncomfortably aware she had been caught staring. "Relax, Mandy. Do your best at the audition, and I will call you the minute I hear anything."

Mandy pushed herself up from the deep cushions, once again the self-assured woman who had first entered the office. China watched as Mandy brushed Reeve's arm in passing, her sounds of appreciation a feminine purr.

The oyster-colored jacket that matched China's wool skirt was draped around her chair. She threw it on, then approached Reeve Laughlin. Offering her slender hand, she felt it swallowed up in his large warm clasp. "Hello, Mr. Laughlin."

"Ms. Payne." For a brief moment he felt as if those wide, charcoal eyes were the windows to her soul. Then silver shutters slammed shut and he could see nothing. She tried to pull her hand out of his but Reeve wasn't giving it up just yet. He looked her over, much to her obvious impatience. She was one perfect lady, he thought. Too perfect! She could use a little mussing up. Strip off that ultrafeminine blouse, scrub away the perfectly applied makeup, and tousle that unruffled hair and, Reeve thought, China Payne might be found. A woman made of flesh and blood—warm flesh, pulsing blood.

"Are you ready, Mr. Laughlin?" The embrace of his eyes was nearly as warm as the hand that still held hers. And then, before she knew his intentions and could step away, he put his mouth on her lips and softly kissed her.

"Why . . . why did you do that?" China whispered.

"Don't family members usually kiss hello?"

"Fam—" She snatched her hand back, angry at his gall *and* his insolent smile. "I am not your family!"

China spun around and walked out of the office. "I'll be back within the hour, Marce," she announced.

For such a brief kiss, China thought, it had packed a powerful punch. At a fast pace she breezed through Marce's small cubbyhole and out to the larger blue and white reception room and didn't stop to look at Reeve until she was out of the building and standing on the street.

Reeve cupped her elbow and walked her toward a burgundy Porsche curbed in a no-parking zone. The hood was up to fake car trouble, and a maintenance man from her building was standing over it with a jug of water. As soon as he saw Reeve he dropped down the hood.

"Thanks, son," Reeve said, rounding the car and tossing a tip to the boy.

"No sweat," the boy replied as he opened China's door. "Anytime."

When China gave Reeve the address of her mother's West Side apartment, his dark brows shot up, and his sideways glance held genuine surprise. It was a well-known building. Residence there demanded great wealth, promised colorful personalities, and implied eccentricities. He sped the car away from the curb and China dug her fingers into the seat leather.

He saw her tense up at his driving and smiled. "Have you been able to find out what this is all about?"

"No. I tried calling the apartment, but the service is taking messages." Then she added unnecessarily, but with wicked pleasure, "Probably to prevent your calls from getting through."

A grunt of disgust was his only comment.

He drove like a slalom skier going too fast on the downslope; speeding from lane to lane, into and out of empty pockets, moving with frightening abandon through clogged streets. Saved by a red light, China relaxed for a moment before the race went into the next lap.

Her eyes were drawn to his bold features. She told herself it was the interest of an agent and nothing else that kept pulling her gaze to his profile.

"You're staring," he said. The arrogant set of his mouth said he was used to it.

"I was thinking I could use you in print work," China explained. "You have good bones, a chiseled profile that photographs well, and a suggestive look women drool over. You could convince them they had to have whatever you were selling."

He laughed, and the rich sound filled the car. "Chiseled? The only chiseled profiles I've ever seen are those four guys on Mount Rushmore. Are you saying I remind you of them?"

China nodded. "Somewhat. They may not be handsome in the 'pretty boy' sort of way, but they are a magnificent spectacle, not to mention breathtaking and quite unique. I'd take them on, too, if I could get an exclusive contract with them."

His first reaction was puzzlement, then utter male arrogance. "Are you interested in me, China?"

Heavens! His ego was so big, she half expected the buttons of his navy vest *and* the white linen shirt to pop. "Oh, I'd take my ten percent, Mr. Laughlin. I wouldn't express any interest if I didn't think you'd earn it for me."

He took his eyes off the road, not advisable as they were off again. "You'd like ten percent of me? Not more? Say twenty percent? Maybe even a hundred?"

"Ten percent of anyone is plenty. Any more and the next thing I know, they expect me to put food in their mouths and be available at midnight. I'll take my ten percent and keep my distance."

"Perceptive of you," Reeve said. "Only I'd expect a hell of a lot more than meals and midnight for *any* percentage of me."

It was the right moment to have arrived at her mother's apartment house. The doorman rushed to China's side and helped her out of the car, then shadowed her steps to the building's brass doors. Just before stepping inside, she saw the hood of the Porsche snap open. He had an unbelievable ego to think the no-parking restrictions applied to everyone in New York but him.

Well, Mr. Laughlin, you've gotten away with far too much already! With a few words to the doorman China made sure Reeve would have to park "legally."

She waited in the lobby, smiling, and feeling a little less as though a bulldozer had torn into her life when Reeve Laughlin had barged into her office. He finally entered the lobby, raking his fingers through his windswept hair.

China called for the elevator as Reeve growled out, "Very good, Ms. Payne."

She glanced from him to the UP button she had just pressed. "Nothing to it. Any five-year-old could have done it just as well."

"I'm talking about your message to the doorman. I'll concede round two to you."

"Two? What was round one? And need I ask who took that?"

"I took the first round . . . the easy way."

Reeve followed China into the car. She pushed the button for the sixth floor and turned to Reeve. "I hope you're ready for this, Mr. Laughlin."

They didn't have to ring the doorbell. Milly had been alerted by the desk and the carved mahogany swung open on a simple marble foyer. It was the only simple, uncluttered space in the whole apartment.

"Come in, Miss China," Milly said. "You too," she grunted at Reeve. China gazed down at the top of Milly's white head. The old woman had been with Clare from the time China was a small girl, and even then China had thought her to be an ancient relic.

Milly's pale, rheumy eyes peered up the long sweep of stairs to the second floor. "She's up there. Don't 'spect she'll be down the rest of this week. She tied one on last night, she did. And you know your mum don't like to drink alone. Now poor Fred has a mighty hangover."

"Fred! She drank with Fred?"

"Yep. Go on up. I'll bring the coffee." Milly shuffled off, muttering as she went. "Y'all be ringing for the booze shortly though. I 'spect y'all be needing it."

China forgot all about Reeve as she ran up the stairs. At the top was a large square hall with three doors behind which were bedrooms with private baths. The upper foyer was richly hung with exquisite oil paintings and a generous ocean-blue sofa was pushed against a white wall. China walked up to the sofa and looked down at the droopy face of her mother's dog, a brown and white basset hound.

Crouching to sit on her heels, she put her face up to his. "You'll get in tons of trouble if you're found up on this sofa." She softly massaged the skin behind his ears. He gazed up at her and let out a small whimper. "Poor

Fred," China crooned. "Hangover? Let that be a lesson to you next time."

Another painful whimper worked its way out of the suffering dog, and China stood up to face a stunned Reeve Laughlin.

"Is that Fred?" he asked in amazement.

"Yes. Not at his best today, as you can see."

"Your mother got drunk with a dog last night?" He shook his head. "Just what kind of nut is she anyway?"

"I don't know, Mr. Laughlin. What variety does your father prefer?"

His face whitened under his tan. "Very good. Not only do you play the game, you play it well."

China turned away from him, reaching for the door to her mother's bedroom. Just before swinging it open, she turned back to Reeve. "Oh, Mr. Laughlin, you ain't seen nothin' yet."

Clare's bedroom always caused an unnerving jolt to China's senses. The whole apartment was erratically creative. There was a boldly lacquered Chinese living room that opened with jarring opposition on a delicate French dining room. The race across centuries was dizzying as a few paces carried one from an Ancient Egyptian anteroom to an Early American library.

The master bedroom lacked a definite theme. Awash in peach satin and black lace, the only period China could liken it to was the sort found at the end of a sentence—her forward progress suffered an enforced stop before she was able to continue.

Today the shades were pulled behind the curtains of the long windows, that, when bared, provided a peaceful view of Central Park. China touched the wall switch to bring up the dimmed lights. It was a huge, high-ceilinged room, nearly as large as China's whole apartment.

Clare was lounging on the bed, on a mountain of

peach satin pillows. Her matching peach eyepatches were fringed in the same black lace that edged the quilted spread, the bed's canopy, and the dozen pillows.

"Good afternoon, Mother," China called.

Clare removed her eyepatches, tipped her head, and smiled. Her swept-up hair, lighter than her daughter's raven thickness, was a warm chestnut streaked with a single, off-center wave of silver. Her eyes, however, were the same charcoal gray as China's. She was fifty-nine years old and could easily have passed for ten years younger.

"Hello, darlings," Clare sang out.

Reeve couldn't believe it. Assuming a casual stance, he slid his hands into his hip pockets as he scrutinized the bordello-type decor. Did his father actually sleep in this room? He tried to imagine Martin shedding his clothes and sliding into a bed so soft, it would fold around a man's weight and suffocate him in his sleep.

"Mother, this is Reeve Laughlin," China began. The introduction was broken off, interrupted by Milly's shuffling entrance. She carried an ornate silver tray laden with refreshments. China stepped forward to take the heavy burden from Milly and slid it to a central table. The unmistakable fumes of brandy rose up from one cup to sting China's nostrils. Concern drew her brows together. Her mother had never before been a habitual drinker—just a terribly outrageous one!

Clare saw China react and immediately defended the bracing splash. "Just some hair of the dog that bit me, dear."

Taking the spiked cup to her mother, China glared down at her. "Speaking of dogs. Fred is sick and miserable and it's your fault. Getting him drunk is the meanest stunt you've ever pulled. And if you even think of doing it again, I'll take that dog away from you."

China heard Reeve chuckling deep in his chest.

Apparently he found the situation funny. But then he hadn't had to live with it for the last thirty years.

"I didn't think he'd actually drink it," Clare protested. "After all, you'd think nature would protect animals with an aversion to alcohol. But I was alone, Joey was gone, Milly was on her night off and . . . Fred was . . . here."

China turned back to the table. Suddenly she needed to busy her hands before she gave in to temptation and wrapped them around Clare's neck. She loved her mother completely; she didn't understand her at all.

Reeve leaned forward for the creamer, brushing her arm in the process. "And who is Joey?" he whispered. "The cat?"

"My brother. Joey is thirteen years old and away at military school. He's my half brother actually, by her third husband."

"My God! What number is my father?"

"Fifth." China swept her arm out indicating the bed and finished the introduction. "Mr. Laughlin, my mother: Clarissa Marie Howard—Mitchell Payne Jeffries Doran Laughlin."

There was a tense moment of silence before Reeve took two steps towards the bed and said, "Now, then, Clare—"

But Clare wasn't even looking at him. *"Mr. Laughlin?"* she snapped. "Really, China, must you be so formal? The man is your stepbrother, after all."

"A fact neither of us was aware of until this morning."

"We're getting off the track here, aren't we?" Reeve interjected.

But Clare, once sidetracked, was not one to retrace her steps, but stubbornly, gleefully, thrash her way down uncharted paths. "Still, he isn't a stranger. It wouldn't hurt you to be more familiar with him. This standoffish attitude of yours is why you're not married again, dear. What's the harm in being friendly with Reeve?" Clare brazenly looked the man up and down. "You could do worse. And he's quite handsome, hmm? Don't you agree, China?"

"Yes, handsome," China agreed, knowing a protest would be useless. "Not to mention magnificent, breathtaking, and unique."

Clare was stunned into silence and she gaped at Reeve's impatient figure. "Why, Reeve, China *never* says such wonderful things about men. She's always so straitlaced and sensible. What did you do to fire the girl up?"

"He was already solicited by me on the ride over, Mother."

"Solicited!" Clare shrieked. "How marvelous, dear. And I was beginning to give up hope."

Seeing those matchmaking eyes shimmer with delirious pleasure, China continued, "Well, you can go on hoping. Reeve turned me down." She turned to look at him. "Didn't you?"

His sideways glance was slightly amused, and the force of it sent a curious tingle through China. Then he met Clare's bewildered gaze. "Her financial arrangements were not to my liking."

"Oh, dear heaven," China moaned.

"What?" Clare screamed.

Reeve looked back at China, one of his brows slanted at a daring angle. My Lord, she thought, he's actually enjoying this! Reeve then grabbed a chair and moved it to Clare's bedside while China distanced herself by going to the window and leaning on the wide sill.

"It seemed a slip of the tongue, Martin's mentioning you," Clare was saying. "For some reason we were speaking of China's divorce, and Martin said, 'When my son divorced . . .' Then he choked up. I couldn't get another word out of him. But it was clear the two of you were estranged. Otherwise I'd have had you to dinner."

China let the words fade to a drone, too busy looking past the bone, blood, and muscle composition of the man sitting next to her mother. The special lighting that flattered Clare's features complimented Reeve with a sensual indulgence. A profile that had seemed hammered out of inflexible bronze by daylight was now an artist's sculpture shaped by sensitive fingers. The forbidding angles that defined his jaw and forehead were tempered, encouraging a woman's touch. But the force of his aggression could not be dampened by clever lighting or muted voices. He's dangerous, China!

And divorced. She didn't think him a man to take anything unless he were very sure he wanted it, and once possessing it, he would be hard put to let it go. She felt a feminine flutter in the center of her being and was appalled. Rather than shrink from his overwhelming presence, she intensified her study. His chiseled mouth had a harsh set when he wasn't smiling. His blue eyes were bright, but the brilliance was chilling, and not likely to flame with warm regard. She shuddered, hoping to shake off the budding attraction.

"He's run off," Clare cried. China forced herself back to the conversation. Reeve's reaction was unreadable; he was probably a superb deadpan in the courtroom, she thought. China guessed that, while he might not have known this, he wasn't very surprised by it. "And robbed me blind," Clare finished.

"I see." Reeve sighed and stood up.

"Stole from me." Hurt and bewilderment made Clare's words quaver.

Reeve shook his head. "This has nothing to do with me."

"But you must find him," Clare demanded. "Immediately."

"Hire a private detective," Reeve said. "Lawyers do not look for runaway husbands."

"I know that." Clare laughed girlishly. "But lawyers do take people to court. If you have to hire a private detective, then do so, and put it on my tab. But I want you to find Martin and get my money."

"No," Reeve abruptly refused. "Get yourself another lawyer. I washed my hands of Martin years ago for exactly this sort of thing, although you are the first one he bothered to marry. If you hadn't lied to me about his life being in danger, I never would have come here today."

"Lie! I never lie. Do I, China?" Clare was stricken by the accusation and turned to her daughter to defend her.

There was a moment of expectant silence; the only sound was the clipped drumming of China's fingernails on the wooden sill. China sighed. "Mother, why don't you tell Mr. . . . uh, Reeve, what sort of danger Martin is in."

Clare fished under the covers of her bed and pulled out a magazine. "Do you see this?"

Reeve bent forward to glance at the title. "*Soldier of Fortune,*" he read. "A magazine for mercenaries."

"That's right," Clare said. "Either you find Martin, Reeve, or I will hire one of these men to find him for me."

The blood seemed to drain from China's head. Mercenaries, Reeve had said. Men paid to go to hot spots in the world and wage war. China stood up, her spine rigidly erect.

"Say what you mean, Mother," China pleaded.

"Guns for hire," Clare stated. She tossed this off as easily as if she were telling Milly to hire Chef Henri to cater a dinner party.

"Hired to do what?" China asked weakly. Her eyes

grew large with horror, her mouth dry, and her tongue felt as if it were coated with sandpaper.

"To shoot, China. Glory be, what else would they do?"

Reeve sank back to the chair at the side of the bed. "This is a joke, isn't it? You're talking about murder! Having my father murdered?"

"It's up to you to prevent it," Clare said. "Find Martin."

No one noticed China. She was in such shock, she could hardly feel her feet touch the floor as she crossed the carpet to stand at the foot of the bed. Her arms hung limply at her sides, her fingertips brushed a soft pillow.

Her voice was a croak. "You've gone mad."

Clare flustered with indignation. "It isn't like you to be rude, China."

"You're crazy," China gasped.

Reeve watched China as her desperate hands crushed a soft pillow to her stomach. He looked at Clare's smoky gray eyes, seemingly devoid of sanity, then into China's swirling depths as she tried to hang on to hers.

Two

"Let's go, China." Reeve tugged the strangled pillow from her hands and tossed it back to the bed.

"You've gone too far this time," China cried at Clare. "You *are* crazy! And this is just plain criminal!"

"China," Reeve began in a husky, soothing voice. His arm moved around her shoulders, drawing her to the support of his strong length. It had been a long time since China had leaned on anyone. His face was an inch from her own. The gentle kindness in his eyes helped to slow the frantic race of her thoughts. "Let's go, China. You're too worked up to do anything about this right now."

"I am not *worked* up." China shot her gaze back to the bed, and the sight of Clare, calmly smiling, seared through the blinding, angry fog. "I am *fed* up."

"China, China," her mother trilled. "Relax, dear. Reeve will take care of everything for us. You'll see."

China put her hands to Reeve's chest and pushed out

of his arms, willing her tears not to fall while he could see them. She didn't want Reeve Laughlin or anyone else taking care of them. One look at his narrowed eyes and tightly set mouth and China knew he was actually giving serious consideration to Clare's ludicrous scheme.

"If you're smart, you'll stay out of this." China singled Reeve out with one pointed, waving finger. "She's playing one of her games. The rules are made up as she goes along. Not even the *best* players beat Clare when she calls the shots."

He took a deep breath and she sensed an argument coming. "Don't say anything," China warned. "Just . . . just take me back to my office, please." She turned to Clare. "Mother"—Clare smiled prettily at China—"I have to leave for the West Coast tonight and won't return until Tuesday. Please, *please*, don't do anything desperate in the next four days, like . . . like contacting the local hit man." Sadness softened China's gaze. "Oh, Mom. How could you waste this man's time with such insanity? Don't you know that you make us look like a pair of fools?"

Pressing her cool palms to the angry heat in her cheeks, China left the bedroom and raced down the stairs. Milly was waiting at the bottom, sitting in a decorative gilt chair. On a nearby table was a tray crowded with crystal decanters, elaborately cut glasses, and an ice-filled bucket.

"I'll bet that was a shocker," Milly said, standing up. "I got the 'tonics' ready. You look like you need one."

"I don't need a drink," China retorted. "Pour it down the sink. And then dump out every last bottle in the house."

Reeve appeared at the top of the stairs, clucking his tongue and shaking his head. "You'll give Fred's affliction to all the sewer alligators." His smile for China as he took the last step was warm and strangely comforting.

Then he turned to Milly. "Do you have a cabinet where you can lock up the liquor? I agree with China that Clare sober will be enough of a handful."

When Milly was gone, Reeve took China's hands in his and she held tightly to his curled fingers. She let her gaze travel up his tie and over his face until she met compassion in his blue eyes. "I'm so . . . sorry," she whispered. Never before had she been ashamed of Clare, embarrassed to claim the woman as her mother. Never before had another person's opinion mattered to her the way Reeve's did at that moment.

"For what? Today?" He cocked his head and fine smile-lines etched his bronze skin. "You don't have to be sorry. This wasn't your doing. As for your mother, I think she's delightful."

"Delightful!" China pulled her hands free and turned to wrench open the front door. "*Delightful*. Oh, God help us," she muttered, stepping into the elevator.

The sidewalk bustled with afternoon traffic and a crisp, skirt-lifting breeze carried the scent of autumn. Reeve marched past her, tossing out "This way," and China remembered he had had to park somewhere else. He didn't slow his pace one bit to make allowances for her feminine stride, and China clenched her teeth at each pinch of her fashionably styled heels. Of the many regrets this day had brought her, that little power-play of managing to have Reeve's low-slung sports car parked blocks away was climbing to the top of the list.

As she spotted the Porsche she saw a fluttering ticket neatly tucked under the windshield wiper. The one-hour parking meter had run out.

"The one time I park legally, I get a ticket," Reeve grumbled. He vented his anger by crushing the ticket in one large, forceful fist.

As they retraced the route they had come China pressed her fingertips to her temples, trying to push back the painful ache building to migraine intensity. Reeve's whistling some happy, carefree tune didn't help. What did she expect from Martin's son? Rational behavior?

Availing himself of the services of her maintenance man once again, Reeve guided her to her building. "I have to use your office phone," he explained. "I'm going on to my next appointment from here and I need to let my secretary know."

They stood with a dozen others at the elevator bank as China sarcastically simpered, "*Please*, China, will you come to your mother's with me? *Please*, may I use your phone, China?" The expression she turned to him was anything but sweet. "Have you ever heard that word— *please*?"

"Yes. And I even use it. But only when I'm offering the option of a yes or no answer. I am not, nor have I so far, given you a choice."

Reeve was eye-to-eye with her, and he arrested a knee-jerk reflex at the broiling storm in those gray depths. The assemblage shuffled forward, piling into the open elevator car until there seemed to be no more room.

"Go ahead. Use Marce's phone," China suggested when the group compressed to make room for one more. "I'll wait for the next one."

Reeve rested a splayed hand on the casing, jamming the withdrawn doors and causing them to hiccup in their attempts to close. "Get in," he ordered. "There's room for both of us."

"No. It will be over the limit."

"I said, get in."

"I said no!"

China had an audience-perfect view of the people squashed together in the elevator—staring, squirming, and waiting. The door hiccuped. The people grumbled. China gave up and got in.

Forced up against Reeve, she felt his hard chest shaking moments before the rich laughter rumbled out of him. She shot him a warning glare, and he made a serious but unsuccessful attempt to hold his laugh back.

"Murder isn't funny," China ground out through clenched teeth.

"Murder isn't likely to happen either." At her floor he followed her out and down the hall. "Come on, China, you don't believe Clare is going to kill Martin."

China threw her hands up helplessly and shook her head. Marce fell in step with the couple entering the inner office. China indicated her desk phone, and Marce gaped as Reeve punched out a number with such enthusiasm he literally had to chase it across the slick surface of China's desk.

When he finished, Marce slid a dubious look at China, then began reading from her note tablet. "The Barstow Company is casting a little girl missing her two front teeth. And there's an audition Monday for a national commercial. They're looking for your standard, plaid-blouse housewife—preferably a blonde."

"Fine. Bring me the blond head-shots in our files. As for the little girl, at what age does a kid lose her front teeth?"

"My nephew just lost his and he's seven," Marce offered.

Reeve wrapped up his business and thoughtfully studied the office decor while China was busy. It was a pleasant room accented with personal touches and unposed photos. She had, Reeve noticed, a penchant for flowers: silk bouquets, a glass sculpture of tulips, a hunk of marble carved down to a delicate rosebud. His gaze settled on a black and white chessboard standing on the walnut coffee table.

"Pull the seven-year-olds," China told Marce, "and start calling their mothers." Marce left and China rushed after her with another thought. "Should it happen that little Martha Marks is seven, *don't* call her mother. Mrs. Marks is liable to knock the poor child's teeth out if it'll get her kid in front of a camera."

When she turned back to Reeve, he was holding one of her chess pieces. "Do you play?"

"Not only do I play the game," she replied, quoting his previous words. "I play it well."

"My move—for winning round one." White always taking the lead, Reeve advanced his white King Pawn two squares.

China glanced at the playing board. His opening move was a basic one. She advanced her black King Pawn one square for her round-two victory. With a nod of his head Reeve left. But he'd be back—China decided, unsure if she liked the idea or not—if only to win the game.

She let herself into her apartment actually looking forward to putting three thousand miles between her and New York. She dropped her keys in a bowl on the white Formica counter in the kitchen, the first room to the left of her front door. Her wool jacket was peeled off as she intersected the all-white living room and stepped into the all-white bedroom. China's apartment was not inspired with much color and even less influenced by her personality. The few rooms were easily coordinated, quickly cleaned, and indifferently left each morning.

A suitcase lay open on the bed, interrupting the snowy expanse. Half filled with crushable clothes, it lay in wait for the less resistant fabrics. She stripped in her bedroom, passed a full-length mirror without a glance at her long-legged nudity, and spun the taps in the bathtub.

She bathed in a state of distraction. She scrubbed a tough-bristle brush over the soles of her feet, mentally reviewing her California itinerary—filling her head with details instead of Reeve Laughlin's shadowy silhouette. Still, the recurring flash of the man's musky scent and radiant blue eyes rippled over her nerves. Washing her hair, she gave up trying to distract her errant senses and let the force of the hot spray drum out that resonant baritone voice.

Why now? He wasn't even here, yet he was more vital than when he had been so near, she'd felt the warmth emanating from his body. She remembered there being more breathing space in the compact car—when it was filled with all that man—than she could find right now.

Damn! Why hadn't he maliciously turned on Clare for the ridiculous scene played out that afternoon? Why couldn't he have ranted and raved and stalked off? Why had he done everything so right, making China feel so damn grateful for his understanding?

She pulled a thick, forest-green robe from the closet and gazed unseeing at the waiting suitcase. Did she have some inherent weakness for stepbrothers? Self-centered, undependable stepbrothers? Paul Doran had not had Clare's outrageous streak. He had courted society's expectations of a respectable doctor, shunning the slightest hint of eccentric behavior. And for that reason China had never guessed at his self-serving nature. Clare and Paul. Neither one ever gave a thought to the consequences others suffered at their hands, China mused. It bordered on masochism that she had married a man so like the mother that nearly drove her mad. It frightened her out of trusting her own instincts.

And, like Clare's long list of husbands, China had baled out when she could no longer take it. That instinct, at least, had been sound.

She shivered and went to close the drapes at the window. With her hand on the drawstring she looked down from her second-floor window at the pedestrians on the street. Hand-holding couples moved with long, easy strides as they smiled into each other's eyes, sharing a special warmth. Solitary figures huddled and scurried through the briskly cold night, rushing to faraway sanctuary. If they smiled at all, it was hidden by heads bent down by the wind.

Her hand dropped away from the drawstring, and China wrapped herself up in her own arms. Despite her toasty apartment, thinking of Clare—remembering Paul—had caused a block of ice to form on her heart. Then from the periphery of her thoughts, Reeve Laughlin appeared to burn off the chill. The devil himself, China decided ruefully. How else could a man with glacial eyes and a chilling demeanor create such a thaw?

Yanking the drapes shut, she slammed the door on further fantasies of Reeve Laughlin.

As hectic and fragmented as the weekend in Hollywood turned out to be, her resolve not to think of Reeve failed miserably. The Saturday-night banquet in support of a worthy charity should have been a dazzling reminder that men such as Reeve Laughlin—the strong, silent, seductive type—abounded. Instead, the Hollywood heroes who personified the sensual stereotype on the silver screen proved to be disillusioningly human. Dressed to perfection for their images, they were all there—beautiful women in hand, individual failings intact.

Throughout the long days and nights, whether she was at the hotel pool, or a working lunch, or a lawyer's office, repeated reminders of *him* popped up. Unexpected encounters with men who had dark, intriguing looks, or a gritty baritone voice, or the casually powerful stride of Reeve Laughlin. Never did all these provocative qualities appear in the same man. The baritone voice was wiry and skittish. And the man with the smooth, prowling gait turned around and China saw a face bloated by liquid meals and eyes bloodshot from parties till dawn.

There seemed to be only one Reeve Laughlin.

China went directly to her office from the airport for the last two hours of Tuesday's workday. Marce produced the list of toothless little girls and the clients sent up the day before to audition for the everyday housewife. China shuffled through the newest batch of unsolicited headshots delivered with the morning mail, glancing over the biographies glued to the backsides. The black-and-white eight-by-ten glossies were handed back to Marce to file.

"China?" Marce said. "Two more things . . . both Reeve Laughlin."

Gray eyes rolled up from studying a letter, and her hunched shoulders tensed. "Why not! Only Reeve Laughlin could be *two* things."

"First—this." She handed over Reeve's bill for services rendered. China had followed through with her promise to bill Reeve for one hour of her time. As an agent, her livelihood depended on a percentage of her clients' professional income. Arriving at an hourly rate had involved some creative figuring. With a swell of satisfaction she had caught the office boy in time for Friday's last mail pickup, wishing she could have seen Reeve's face when he opened it.

Now she held a return bill. She glanced down and gasped at how valuable he considered his time. She had a very cynical thought at the sort of services she'd have to perform to be worth that much. He had cleverly subtracted her bill from the balance and penciled a notation that he would put the outstanding balance on Clare's tab. At the very bottom he had coded his next chess move—P–Q4. He was advancing his Queen Pawn.

China crumpled the invoice in her fist. "What is the other?"

"He's been calling all day. Wants you to go to dinner with him tonight."

"Call him back and tell him no."

Ten minutes later Marce poked her head into the office. "Mr. Laughlin again. He wants to speak with you."

China shook her head.

"I'm supposed to tell you he needs to update you on your mother's case."

He was taking it, then. Helping in his own father's prosecution—if he managed to find him. "Tell him Clare can do that herself."

Marce left the connecting door open and China leaned forward, trying to eavesdrop. She couldn't make out the words, but she did see Marce lay the phone down on her desk blotter instead of hanging up. "Mr. Laughlin has asked me to say—let's see if I can do this the way he did." Marce drew the next word out earnestly. "Pleeaassse."

China laughed out loud. Please. He was giving her a choice. She lifted her receiver and Marce left the room. "You can pick me up at eight o'clock," she announced.

"Welcome back, China. Have a good trip?" His low-pitched voice brought a smile to her lips.

"I'll tell you all about it at dinner, Reeve."

"It's amazing what a little *pleasing* will get you." The heavy dose of suggestion he gave the word convinced China of the fortune he could make doing voiceovers.

"All it got you is a dinner date. However, I get another chess move. You can advance my Queen Pawn two spaces also."

Her chessboard had been put back to Opening Position by the weekend cleaning crew. China brought the game up to date with the four moves, then penned a note that she placed on the center of the board: DO NOT TOUCH.

From her window overlooking the street, China saw Reeve pull up. The unleashed power of the Porsche announced him by rattling the window casings. Parked cars lined both sides of the street; if he double-parked, the street would be impassable. One questioning brow lifted as China watched him back up to the corner. He gently eased the front tires over the curb *and drove down the sidewalk*, parking at her front door.

"He's crazy," China muttered.

His knock on her door had all the firm demand of his forceful personality. China opened it to him and was rewarded for her earlier efforts to dazzle him by the sucking gasp of Reeve drawing a breath. He angled his shoulder to the jamb and, without even entering her small foyer, managed to fill it with his presence.

"I knew there was a flesh and blood woman under the lady."

China's knees weakened as his eyes traveled over her with the intimate languor a man might use to view a life-size nude.

The deep V neck of her long-sleeved waist-cinching dress flattered every swell and curve of her statuesque figure. The unusual shade of the stormy blue silk coaxed her eyes to a luminous gray-blue. Reeve leaned forward, taking a breath of her perfume, inhaling its fragrant promise.

"Mmm, nice," he murmured.

Sensations swamped China, and she moved back a step, out of the danger zone. "Isn't it against the law to park on the sidewalk?"

"I'm not sure." He grinned. "I specialize in corporate taxes."

When she stepped away from the door to get her coat from the closet, he walked into her apartment. His coffee-brown suit fit the tapering of wide shoulders to lean hips with the perfection of custom tailoring. She passed over her black linen evening coat twice before finding it.

Satisfying his curiosity about where she lived, he stood in the archway of the living room, slowly canvassing the antiseptic space. Then his eyes met hers from over his shoulder. "How long have you lived here?"

"Three years," China said. "Since my divorce." The collar of his cream shirt deepened the tan of his coppery flesh, and his eyes were so blue, it was sinful. She'd been wrong about those eyes. Not only could they light with warm regard—they could flame!

Reeve looked once more around the white expanse. A bottle of bleach couldn't have done a better job of washing out distinction, he thought. Not a single personal item in sight. The walls were starkly bare, with only an occasional lampshade rising up to relieve the austerity. Glass tables served the purpose of supporting functional lamps. She might have lived here for three years, he thought; she had not, however, moved in yet.

"Ready?" Reeve asked. He helped her into her coat, the unruffled spill of her black hair blending with the fabric. His fingers curled around her arms from behind; time and China's heart stood still until a forward step set the world right again. Her silver clutch purse lay on the edge of a table and Reeve picked it up for her as she bent to snap off the lamp. She had turned on the stove-top light earlier so she wouldn't return to a dark apartment, and its faint flickering glow crept out from the kitchen providing unearthly illumination.

Both of them turned at once from opposite directions,

Reeve's muscled body trapping China in a hallway corner. He put his hands to the wall at either side of her head and chewed thoughtfully on his lower lip. The cool plaster at her back was in direct opposition to the body heat of the man in front of her. His hand resting near her temple and the hard-boned fingers that held her delicate satin purse drew her gaze. It was a riveting sight— Reeve crushing something of hers that was soft and personal.

His words were quiet and suggestive. "Advantage, Laughlin." Her gaze jumped to his face. Lambent flames heated the sapphire eyes, and she narrowed hers instinctively.

"You're confusing your tennis with your chess," China replied. She had intended the words to be cool and impassive. She heard her own voice land between them . . . too husky, too breathless.

"I don't care what the name of the game is . . . so long as we play."

"We'll play Mother May I, then," China said, stalling his kiss.

"May I?"

"No, you may not."

His mouth kicked into a wry grin as he stepped back, and the charged moment was diffused. On the landing and down the narrow flight of steps China felt Reeve's eyes on her. She sensed his approval that she hadn't eagerly fallen into his arms and wondered if he knew how much iron will she'd had to call on not to.

As he tucked her into the passenger seat he murmured, "You won that round, China. You're quicker than I gave you credit for."

"Does that earn me a chess move? It's not my turn, you know. It's your move next."

"Oh, I'll make a move . . . soon." The soft thud of the

door closing echoed the sound of her heart dropping to her feet.

China decided she could read Reeve's moods by the way he drove. He had sped with daring and impatience to her mother's, then returned to China's office with thoughtful caution. Now he drove with nonchalant skill, relaxed in his soft leather bucket seat, one hand resting on the steering wheel. China was sure he viewed the next few hours with equal self-confidence.

"West Side Russian?" she questioned as Reeve held the door open at the Russian Tea Room. "I had you pegged as an East Side French man."

"Did you? You'll lose the game if you start pigeon-holing me."

Had he chosen this restaurant to mislead her? Chess was a game of strategy, of weighing and judging. It didn't hurt to know your opponent well and keep a few steps ahead. Very good, Counselor, she gloated, deciding the restaurant was a smoke screen—until they were led to their table. Circling the tables jammed too close together on the floor, they were shown to a more private, red-leather banquette. The preferred seating said Reeve was a regular and valued customer. He was consistently out of character for the roles China cast him in. People who threw away the script and ad-libbed their lives made China very uneasy.

Obviously she wasn't showing Reeve the impressed delight he expected. "Don't look so disappointed, China. Next time East Side French. I'll take you to Lutèce."

Drink orders were taken and menus laid in front of them. His promise of a next time sent her heart rocketing around her rib cage; it was just the sort of internal shaking up she needed. He had the draw of a magnet. However, she had long ago sworn off men—women too— who could not be depended on to be dependable. Being a West Side Russian man wasn't such a big deal. But a long-haired, conservative lawyer who broke the law was another matter.

Grasping at the purpose for this dinner date, China led the conversation to that topic as her wine and his Scotch were set down. "Why have you decided to represent Clare?"

"I have a choice?" He laid the menu down on the table and the waiter rushed back to take their orders. Reeve ordered his favorite, *nalistniki*, for both of them.

"Reeve, you do know that Clare would never hire someone to . . . to . . ." China couldn't say the word aloud. "To do Martin in."

"She *has* hired someone to do Martin in," Reeve argued, then hurried on when the blood drained from her face. "I don't mean to murder him, China. But hiring the man's very own son to represent her in legal action against him is certainly going to do *something* to Martin."

"Refuse her. You have perfectly good reasons to. Tell her it's conflict of interests, or partiality, or something."

Reeve sat back and gazed at China, peeling the layers away until she felt naked. She clenched her fists under the table to stop a real shiver. "I also have a perfect reason to accept the case. Tell me about your divorce."

China tasted her wine. "Tell me about yours."

"All right." His furrowed brow smoothed out as cold detachment slipped over his face. "We married in my last year of law school. I thought Ann was everything I wanted in a wife. I guess she thought I was everything she wanted in a husband. She was beautiful, sophisticated, and dependent. The perfect lawyer's wife." He sounded as clinically removed as a pathologist describing an autopsy. "I was her ticket out of poverty and into Bendel's and the Four Seasons."

He tasted his Scotch and the clench of a jaw muscle after he swallowed told China the past was not the severed memory implied by his monotone. "I wound up with a wife so helpless that a cookbook and a stove in the same kitchen outnumbered her. Extravagant department store charges piled onto my existing school loans and I studied through a lot of lonely nights while she partied without me."

"And Ann?" China couldn't help asking.

"She got what she was after." His reflexive grimace was harsh. "Ann learned a valuable lesson living with an attorney—get a better lawyer than the other guy has. My illustrious colleague convinced the judge that Ann's sacrifices to put me through law school deserved financial compensation. It was an exorbitant amount for two part-time jobs waitressing. She managed to get fired from both after less than a week. The settlement extended my school loans another five years."

Reeve had made China's mistake, she told herself: Married someone just like the parent that embarrassed him. The first-course salad was placed before them, and Reeve made a quick transfer of attention.

"Your turn," he prompted. It seemed their relationship was destined to progress by turns and moves.

"I didn't say I would tell you about my divorce," China argued.

"Suit yourself. I can always ask Clare."

"Yes, you probably would." China considered that while he speared a bright red tomato with his fork and popped the large portion in his mouth. "His name was Paul Doran."

Reeve's head snapped up and he stared at her. He swallowed and began choking on the uncut tomato quarter.

"God! What happened?" China grabbed his water glass and offered it to him. "Is there something wrong?"

He brought the choking spasm under control. "You said Paul Doran?" His hand slid inside his jacket and produced a packet of folded papers from his breast pocket. Shoving his salad plate to the side, he unfolded the sheets on the table. "Wasn't Clare married to a Paul Doran?" His eyes rapidly skimmed the papers until he found what he was looking for on the third page.

"Here! Husband number four . . . Paul Doran." He dropped back in his seat, the discovery as stunning as a fist to his solar plexus. "My God, you and your mother shared a husband?"

Three

"No!" It never occurred to China that he would so drastically misconstrue things. "Clare was married to Paul Doran, Senior . . . I was married to—"

"Your stepbrother!" Reeve exclaimed. His wide grin slipped into an expression of curiosity. Then even that slipped to wary calculation. "You married your stepbrother?"

"You look like you've just discovered you have symptoms that point to a fatal illness." China laughed. "It's not contagious, Reeve. And he wasn't my stepbrother . . . exactly."

"He and I have more in common all the time. What was he . . . exactly?"

"A doctor, finishing his residency in psychiatry. It wasn't until after we were married that we invited *my* mother and *his* father to dinner. Both of them were single at the time, and Clare, being Clare, did what comes naturally to her. She married Paul's father."

"Did you get divorced together too?" Reeve's question turned her spine into a hot shaft of anger.

"It was unfortunate that when Paul and I had our troubles, our parents took sides. Some might say we got divorced together."

Reeve nodded permission to the waiter to remove his virtually untouched salad; then he ignored his dinner. China considered her *nalistniki* and her mouth watered. The pâté-filled crepes in mushroom sauce were far too tempting to dismiss so lightly.

"And some did say that, didn't they? I remember now. Those divorces got quite a write-up in the papers," Reeve remarked.

China's fork fell from her fingers to the table. "Quite."

"It's been a while," Reeve commented. "I don't remember the details."

China would never forget. The memory of walking out of the courthouse after the divorce was finalized would forever haunt her. The press waiting on the steps, clogging her path, aiming their cameras. "Get a shot of the tears on her face," a reporter had yelled to his cameraman. A quirk of fate, or a judicial secretary with a sadistic sense of humor, had scheduled both Clare and China to divorce their respective Mr. Dorans on the same morning. And hadn't the press had a field day with that. Never again. Never!

Reeve studied her face as a heart-wrenching pain passed over it. "I think I'm beginning to understand you, China."

"Do you? Then you know to drop the subject of my divorce."

"We'll go on with the list. Paul Doran, Senior, wasn't Joey's father." Reeve dropped his eyes to the packet, trying to line up all Clare's husbands in proper order.

China shook her head. "No, that was Dan Jeffries."

"And you're the daughter of her first husband?"

"No. My father was Clare's second husband." Reeve was studying the sheet again, finding Arthur Payne's name. "Would you like me to run through them for you?"

"That might help."

"The case?"

"No," he spoke blandly. "Just help. Now that I'm her lawyer, I'd like to know who I can expect to run up against."

"Oh, none of her husbands, that's for sure. Unless you manage to find your father." China took a breath and began. "I don't know much about her first husband—other than that his name was Roger Mitchell and he was a World War Two soldier killed in action. She has faded photographs of him, a young, blond man in uniform. I was about eight years old when I first found one and asked about him. She wouldn't say a whole lot, but there was a feeling of sadness when she said his name. I guess she loved him and expected my father to fill his army boots."

Reeve allowed her the silence that fell. Suddenly becoming aware of it, China looked up and blinked things back into focus. "Anyway, he couldn't—or wouldn't; and I don't think he should have had to. The marriage lasted a volatile thirteen years and I am their only child. Two years after they—"

"Where is your father now?" Reeve interjected.

China pressed her lips together. She didn't want her father tangled up in Clare's latest snarl. "He lives here in New York."

"Do you see him often?"

"Yes."

"Get along with him?"

"Why?"

Reeve shook his head. "No reason. Just wondering."

"We get along," China murmured. "Two years after

their divorce Clare married Dan Jeffries and they had a son, my half brother, Joey." China stirred cream and sugar into her coffee. "Believe it or not, Clare lost all patience with Dan," she said, then grinned. "Seems the man was too strange for her. Clare found him eccentric, outrageous, undependable . . ."

Even Reeve had to laugh at that. "That *is* hard to believe."

"Believe it. I don't know what chance Joey stands of becoming a level-headed, rationally-thinking adult, considering the unmanageable combination of genes he's got. Last I heard, Dan was the grandfather figure on a California commune, growing organic food and wearing dried lima beans around his neck."

"Then she married your father-in-law."

"Right. It lasted the same two years that my marriage lasted."

"And why did you and Paul break up?" Reeve asked.

China had been hoping they had left the topic of Paul Doran for good. "I thought you were safely led astray."

He shook his head from side to side, his eyes fixed on her masked features. "Old lawyer trick; let the witness relax with the inconsequential. Then pop the unexpected."

Reeve talked China into ordering a peppermint schnapps. The young waiter took their order and moved away, and Reeve waited. "Paul and I had what you might call an idealistic, open-minded marriage. I was naively idealistic, and Paul was unacceptably open-minded." Open minded, open arms, open bedroom door, China thought.

"That's all you're going to say?"

"Old witness trick," China bantered. "Answer only the question asked."

Reeve knew not to push. "How soon after number four did Clare marry my father?"

"Two years? No. Three? You'll have to forgive me if I'm not accurate, but Martin was one of an awfully long list." If the spoon in his hand had been a pencil, it would have snapped in half. China was immediately sorry for the words that caused a dark flush to rise up Reeve's neck. "I'm sorry, that was uncalled for. You've had plenty of opportunity to rub my face in Clare's antics and have been kind enough not to do so. I had no reason to throw Martin up to you." His blue eyes stopped canvassing the room and, when they met her pleading gray ones, he nodded acceptance of her apology.

She was unable to breathe while his gaze assessed her, then seemed to move inside to peer at her soul. "She's hurt you," he said softly.

A hot sting of tears rushed to her eyes, and China blinked furiously to clear them away. "I would think that's obvious."

"I figured you enjoyed her craziness."

"You've got to be kidding!"

"You stick around for it."

"She's my mother, Reeve! My family! I have an obligation to her."

"You have an obligation to yourself," he snapped. He was suddenly angry and China couldn't for the life of her figure out why. "Maybe you stick around for the vicarious spice she gives your life. Hell, China, I don't know why you take it if it hurts you. But if you didn't secretly relish her eccentric behavior, you'd do what I did with Martin—wash your hands of the whole damn mess."

He was so cold now that China wondered if he didn't have a stone where his heart should be. "What about loyalty? Commitment? Love?"

"What about it? Where is Clare's loyalty, commitment, and love? You know the old saying, You choose your friends; your family you get inflicted on you."

"You've misquoted, but your point is made." Sadness filled China. How lonely it would be not to have the permanence of family, even her sort of family. And there was another consequence of Reeve's statement; he as much as said he felt bound to no one. *Wash your hands* of people you love? "Let's get to the business at hand, shall we? You did get me to come out with you so I could hear about Clare's case."

With his head tilted back, his gaze slid over China. He stared at her from the crest of his chiseled cheekbones with undisguised humor. "I got you to come out with me tonight by 'pleasing' you." Sitting up straighter, he was suddenly all business. "Things are rolling, however. I've contacted a private investigator, a man our firm uses often. Shall I give you his background?"

China shook her head. "I wouldn't know what to look for." Never had she felt more like her mother's guardian. It was best to handle it this way though. Two clear-headed adults proceeding in a logical manner. As long as Clare was satisfied that something was being done, there would be no more talk of hit men. Oh, how absurd it all was!

"He's checked with the post office to see if Martin arranged for mail to be sent to a forwarding address. Also the Motor Vehicles Bureau, life insurance companies, banks, et cetera, for a change of address or new accounts. Social Security office on the off-chance that Martin is working. Phone company . . ." The list was endless. Reeve skimmed the papers as he spoke. How did people ever manage to disappear? China wondered. ". . . as expected, none of this has led us to him."

"Why expected? Where is he living? How does he get around? What does he do all day? You make it sound like you can't go to the corner drugstore for a newspaper without being traced."

"If you charge it, we can trace it. So far we have only

In the shadowy interior of his car Reeve began to make his move. Her hand was resting on the center console, and with his free hand he traced the oval shape of her fingernails, the soft flesh of her palm, the delicate veins at her wrist. China rolled her head on the soft leather and stared at his relaxed mouth, so full and appealing. *How will it feel when that mouth covers mine?* With the hunger and passion that was missing from the first soft brush of his lips in her office. Her eyes fell to his long fingers moving over her flesh, waking all her senses.

Warning bells rang in her brain. Instinct told her Reeve would not be a casual involvement. Damn her instinct—afraid to trust it, afraid not to.

"Planning your strategy?" Reeve asked. His voice held as many secrets as the darkened doorways they were passing.

"What strategy is that?"

"To thwart my next move?" Such threatening words said so silkily, quieting her apprehensions. "It won't be long now. Success is going to taste so very sweet, China."

He pulled up in front of her building and killed the motor. The silence was oppressive. China groped for the door handle, then was crushed into her seat by Reeve leaning over to stop her movements. "I'll come around and get you." His lips moved on hers as he spoke, her gaze centered on his pulsebeat throbbing in his temple. He eased away without kissing her. Damn the man! If he meant to build her to a fever pitch so that she was all the more eager, he was—well, he was doing a hell of a good job of it!

The burst of cold air when he opened her door released the shudder China had been holding back. His arm slipped around her waist as they went into the building.

He had to drop back going up the narrow stairs, planting his hands on her hips as he followed her up.

He took the key from China's hand and slid it into the lock. She was pressed to the wall by his body—once again caught between cool plaster and a very warm man.

"How is eight o'clock Friday night?" he asked, unlocking but not opening her door. He was only a breath away from her. His lazy gaze watched her brows draw together in confusion, her teeth nibble at her lower lip. Her mouth was free of lipstick and his eyes followed the natural line of her naked lips. God, she'd be very hard to walk away from. "You remember, China. Lutèce. I promised you East Side French." He unbuttoned her coat, slipping his hand inside to rest under the soft swell of her breast. "And I always keep my promises."

"And if I refuse to go?" she whispered. Her heart jumped in and out of his palm with erratic rhythm.

"Let's not start that again," he growled. "We already played that strategy. Be original."

"Eight-thirty is better," she said with a smile.

"Good." Her eyes were half closed, and she had the heavy, floaty look of a person drugged. He leaned to the left and her door opened. Through the fringe of her lashes she saw his head move, his shoulders turn away. "Good night, China."

He was walking away!

From the top step he glanced back at her. If only she could see herself, Reeve thought. Arms that had hung at her sides slowly came up until her hands were on her hips. And that expression! She looked like a Little League ballplayer who couldn't believe the umpire had called her out.

"What kind of a move is that?" China demanded. But he was relieved to see that she was more baffled than angry.

"A strategic move. Frustrating too. I won this round, China."

She cocked her head to one side. "And just how do you figure that?"

"This time you *didn't* get what you wanted." He turned and went down the stairs while he still could. From the bottom of the stairwell he called up, "Advance my King Pawn, China."

He was gone! China walked into her apartment to stand in the middle of the living room. He'd just left her standing there! She walked to the window, superimposing the chessboard on the ebony glass, and made Reeve's move in her head. Her answering options were very limited; he had effectively prevented the play she planned to make next. The board vanished, and she saw Reeve out on the street looking up at her. He raised his arm in salute and China flung open the window.

"You didn't get the kiss you wanted either, Reeve. Advance my Queen Pawn."

"Friday night, China. Eight-thirty."

She rested her elbows on the sill and watched him drive to the corner, then head south toward home, wherever that was.

Slamming the window shut, she turned away, slapping her hands together in a dusting-off gesture. She had made an excellent move, considering how he had cramped her development.

Then she realized that he was already in command of the game, controlling her play by eliminating her options. Her first step to freedom was on the path he had designated.

Four

"Morning, China," Marce called out as China entered the Payne Agency reception room a half hour earlier than usual.

"Marce! What are you doing here?"

"Just a little behind. Thought I'd catch up while the service is still taking our calls."

Marce's devotion was a true godsend. Not only was she worth her weight in residual checks as a secretary, but she didn't hesitate to pinch-hit as receptionist, bookkeeper, errand girl, or talent scout.

"And you?" Marce asked.

"Oh, you know me," China muttered, peeling off the jacket of her dove-gray suit and hanging it in her closet. "If I'm awake, I might as well be here working."

China yanked her tennis shoes off and dumped them in her bottom desk drawer. Unzipping her tote bag, she pulled out heels that matched her suit, dropping them close enough to her chair to slide them on at a moment's notice. Her shoulders ached with fatigue; it had been a long, restless night of emotional tug-of-war. By the time she drifted into fitful sleep, the vision of Reeve was clinging to her mind in an embrace that her body could only yearn for. As she straightened up, her eyes fell on the morning paper waiting on her desk and folded back to a specific article. Marce always brought them to her attention.

Slinging her purse over her shoulder, Marce slammed an open file drawer shut, announcing, "I'm off to the coffee shop for doughnuts. Want anything?"

China stood rigidly, glaring at the newsprint without reading the words.

"Uh . . . well," Marce hemmed. "So! I'll . . . uh, be back soon."

Alone, China reached for the paper, slowly sinking into her chair as she stared at the bold print. MARTIN LAUGHLIN MISSING? "Oh, no," China groaned. She tried to convince herself that the fact it was a news article on page 3A instead of a gossip column lent it respectability. At least Clare's colorful background was covered without the usual tongue-in-cheek sarcasm. All of her stepfathers were listed with accuracy and brief biographies of China and Joey given. Martin was hardly mentioned!

China stood up and wandered out to the reception room. The quiet was peaceful in an expectant way, as if any minute the five rooms would burst into busy life. She stood at the window watching New York wake up. With her hands clasped behind her she shifted her weight from heels to toes, rocking thoughtfully. Storing up her courage because tomorrow the gossipmongers would take that news bit and make a full meal of it.

Like it or not—and she didn't like it one bit—she realized Reeve had arranged for the article. China felt an immense personal betrayal.

She looked around the alabaster walls covered with

her client's pictures, at the oak tables waxed to a soft sheen, and the sofa and chairs upholstered in a muted blue pattern. She was searching, trying to find the calm security and sense of belonging she always felt here. All she could find was a big hole in her life. A glaring emptiness previously filled by the agency, by her family of actors and actresses, by the wining and dining of advertising firms.

She heard the office door open at her back and turned to see Marce returning with a paper sack full of doughnuts. Marce, who made sure she ate breakfast and kept her appointments. Marce, who fielded her phone calls and brought publicity to her attention. Marce, who took care of China so that China could take care of everyone else. Instead of a man, she had a bouncy, energetic, twenty-two-year-old secretary. Suddenly it wasn't enough.

"China? What is it?" Marce dropped her sack on a convenient table, alarmed at her employer's blank stare. "You look sick, like you're going to pass out."

China forced a weak smile. "It doesn't need me," she murmured. Then she cleared her throat and said with force, "This agency doesn't need me eighteen hours a day, seven days a week, anymore. When I wasn't looking, it got on its feet!"

"I've been telling you that. Haven't you looked at your profit-and-loss statements recently? You're as financially sound as it's possible to be in the entertainment industry."

"My God, Marce, what will I do with all those hours now?"

"Oh, boy. Have I got a cousin for you! He's a knockout."

"No," China firmly refused. "I'm sure he's wonderful. But I swore off the blind-date route when I was in high school. I'll find my own, thanks."

The phone rang and China glanced at her watch— nine o'clock on the button. The door opened and the rest of her staff piled in, and that sleeping vibrancy burst forth. Only it wasn't quite as electric and thrilling as it used to be.

Her first call of the day was from the company casting the new prime-time show Amanda Temple had been sent up for. Ten minutes later she asked Marce to get Mandy on the phone.

Breaking the hold-connection was like dynamiting the dam on Mandy's overflowing excitement. "What is it, China? Did you hear anything? I think I was good. Did I get it? Why haven't they called? I can't stand it! Why don't you say something? . . . I was terrible, wasn't I—"

"Halt!" China laughed into the sudden silence. "You have a callback. They looked at a hundred girls for the part of the governor's mistress, and they've narrowed it down to five. You're still in the running."

China held the phone away from her ear when Mandy began screaming with hysterical delight. Then she gave Mandy the time and place of the second taping before hanging up. Leaning back in her chair, she grinned up at the ceiling. Those were the calls that made her love what she did for a living.

"Look at you—gloating like you won the role yourself," Marce scoffed. "Here, this'll bring you back down to earth." Her arms were wrapped around a stack of mail that she dumped on the coffee table.

China flopped down on her sofa and stretched out with her back to the pillowed armrest and her toes curled under a cushion. "Lord, but I'm tired. Hold my calls while I go through these. And I don't want to see *anybody*."

Marce left the office, pulling the door shut behind her but not hard enough for it to latch. China worked in a cocoon of solitude, listening to the muted sounds of the agency's heartbeat pumping away, keeping them all alive.

Along with bills and head shots, she riffled through pieces of correspondence requiring a personal reply. China was jolted from her deep concentration by the beginnings of a commotion in the outer office. A deep-timbred voice rose and fell. The insistent, higher-pitch had to be Marce trying to keep the man out of China's domain.

"Oh, really," China finally complained. She pushed herself up from the sofa, clutching letters in each hand. She got as far as the center of the room when the door flew open.

"Reeve?" she gasped. Whom was he so mad at? The door had been flung open with such force, and his eyes were shooting blue sparks. But his mouth was smiling as he sauntered in. He stopped an arm's length away from her. "What are you doing here?"

"Trying to get past your watchdog, for one thing," he growled.

"I'm sorry, China. I tried to stop him," Marce huffed from the door.

"It's all right, Marce." Without her shoes on China was a good six inches shorter than Reeve. She had to tilt her head to meet his eyes. The hungry desire there dried her mouth and made her knees tremble.

"You kept me from sleeping last night," he ground out. "And from working this morning too." China couldn't speak at all as he lithely closed the gap between them. "And I thought Clare was a plague."

Then she was hauled to his chest, held there by the clamp of his hands on her upper arms. He gazed down—at her gray eyes, wide and transfixed; at her full mouth, invitingly parted in surprise. "I don't think last night's strategy was worth the consequences."

His mouth covered her parted lips and her eyelashes

fell as wave after wave of a sensual flood washed over her. His tongue intimately plundered the dark hollow of her mouth, licking at every sweet drop. Tunneling into her hair, his large hand positioned her head. He was not harsh or hurtful, yet China was overwhelmingly aware of a leashed urgency, his control over the need to have all of her at once. Her bones quivered like wind-battered twigs while her blood ran to hot liquid. Sheets of white paper fell from her limp fingers to scatter at their feet.

China moaned as the reality of Reeve holding her eclipsed all her imagined fantasies of the night before. That groan of womanly pleasure slammed a shudder through Reeve's hard body. He dragged his mouth from her to speak raggedly, his lips nuzzling her cheek with the words. "That tasted so much sweeter than strategy."

His hands slid from her waist to her bottom, crushing her soft shape to his hard length. Wanting to touch his skin, her hands traveled up his back, frustrated from contact with his warm flesh by his suit jacket. As he nibbled her lips apart to receive his velvet tongue, her hands framed his face, her fingertips buried in his crisp black hair. No longer stunned by Reeve here and kissing her, China actively sought the intimacy of his mouth, running her tongue over his teeth and the soft inner flesh, flicking in and out like a bee after honey.

They clung to each other when it was over. Their foreheads pressed together, eyes locked in wordless wonder. The depth to which they had just lost themselves was profound.

"Well, well," Marce said from the doorway, startling them out of the embrace.

China blinked as Reeve stepped aside, pulling her under his arm. "Have you been standing there all this time?" China asked. Had it been seconds? Longer?

"No one asked me to leave," Marce cheekily replied.

"I'm asking you to leave. Now," China ordered.

Giggling, Marce departed, pulling the door closed behind her. This time China heard the latch click. They stood there. China stared at the closed door, willing her body to return to normal, her pulse to regulate, her breath to draw easy.

Reeve's chuckle broke the strained tension. "Would you believe that same girl shrank away from me last week?"

"Marce does that if she feels personally threatened." China couldn't believe they were having a normal conversation after such an intense moment. "But God help anyone who tries to come after me."

"Well, what did you think?" he asked.

China stepped away from him, pushing his arms away and distancing herself from the overpowering nearness of his all-too-masculine body. Wry humor snapped in her bright eyes even as she feigned surprise. "Oh, was that an audition of some sort? Am I supposed to critique your performance?"

His head reared back on his neck as he glared at her. "I want to know what you think about *us.*"

"I read it all the time. Very good magazine."

"Dammit, China." He was fast losing patience.

That it was so important to him sobered her. "I don't know, Reeve. I haven't had much chance to think about us."

"The hell you haven't. You look like your night was as bad as, if not worse than, mine." The quirk of his mouth announced egotistical satisfaction.

"We've known each other all of five days, and I spent three of those out of town. I hardly know you, let alone what I think of you."

"Fair enough. You can ask me all the questions you want at lunch tomorrow." He flicked his wrist, baring a gold Piaget watch. "Today is already backed up; I'll be working late as it is. How is one o'clock tomorrow?"

She was smiling, nodding her head, convinced she was crazy. "Fine. Where shall I meet you?"

"Come to my office." He stepped up to her, his arms folding around her. "You can see where I work, meet my colleagues, ask my secretary about all my bad habits. I'll even have her type up a résumé for you."

He dropped his head to her shoulder, nuzzling her neck inside the collar of her blouse. "God, you smell good." She felt his attention shift elsewhere and leaned back to look up at his face. He was gazing past her at the chessboard.

"By the way"—he put her to one side and leaned down to pick up the white Queen—"I spoke with Clare this morning." He held the crowned piece up for China to see. "I advised her to get an annulment, and she wants a *month* to think about it." He placed the royal piece up the Queen-Knight file. "I was right. She'll never do it."

China half collapsed, leaning on the chessboard, her eyes closed. She sighed, releasing a great weight with the expelled breath. "Oh, I'm so relieved."

"Hey, there." Reeve tipped her chin up with a gentle finger. "That much relief can't be just because Clare might stay married this time."

"Yes, it is. Last night I started reliving the other times, the snide headlines of the gossip columns, the four inches that follow—so many gory details in so few words. I just don't think I can stand them one more time. 'Clare Howard, Movie Heiress, Dumps Leading Man.' 'Clare Takes Her One-woman Show on the Road Again.' Joey and I are always included in the complicated history. It takes weeks for the talk to die down."

"And here I thought it was want of me that kept you awake last night."

But China wasn't able to respond to the playful bantering. Instead, she picked up that morning's paper, folded to the most recent article. "Did you do this, Reeve?"

He only had to glance at the headline. "Why?"

"You did. How could you? We talked about this kind of thing last night. You must have known—"

"Hold it. This had already gone to press last night."

Of course. She hadn't thought of that. Then he hadn't done it without regard for her feelings. "Promise me you won't do it again."

"China, my father is missing. I have to do what I can to find him."

"Just a minute. Four days ago you had washed your hands of him. And now you have to do whatever you can to find him? Even if you have to use me?"

"It has nothing to do with you!"

"How can you say that?" China hit him on the arm with the rolled paper, venting her frustrated fury. "God knows Clare should provide a smorgasbord of juicy tidbits to fill even the hungriest of scandal-seekers. But no, we're dealing with gluttons, and being Clare's daughter qualifies me to spice up what might otherwise be a stale story. Have you ever opened the morning paper and read where you dined last night, whom you were with, and what you wore? What business is it of theirs and who in the world cares?"

Carpet fibers blurred to a watery blue pond as her eyes filled with tears. "You know what's worse than the garbage they make up? *The truth.* Where do they get it? Do they tap my phones? Hide in my closet? 'According to a source who will remain nameless' means your best friend left a heart-to-heart and played Deep Throat with the newspapers—" A sob prevented her going on.

Reeve brushed a tear away with his thumb and cradled her head to his chest. "Please, Reeve, please. No more articles." He didn't answer, and China tipped her head to look him in the eye. "Reeve?"

"I can't promise, China. I have a job to do, and if I need to use the papers to do it, I will." She went rigid in his arms, and Reeve touched his lips to her smooth forehead. "Cut yourself off from it, China. It can't hurt you if you won't let it."

China looked up at him. How could a man with such warm eyes have such a cold heart? Had he been hurt so deeply in the past that he now washed away and cut off everything that might hurt him in the future?

"Don't look at me like that, China. Like I'm some kind of monster. I'll compromise, okay? I won't use the papers again unless absolutely necessary and I *do* promise not to give out information about you."

China remembered her first impression of Reeve—that he wasn't a man to compromise or negotiate. That he would now seemed a step in the right direction, her direction. She leaned back into his arms, her cheek resting on his chest, believing him simply because she so desperately wanted to.

From where she stood, China had a perfect view of the chessboard and studied Reeve's position. "You sure you don't want to reconsider today's move?"

Laughter rumbled from his chest to her ear. "I most certainly do not!"

She wriggled free of him, rolling her eyes heavenward. "I mean that one." She pointed to the board. "Your Queen is very vulnerable standing out there unprotected from potshots."

"Let me defend my Queen, will you? I've got to go; I'm running behind." He moved to the door. "And don't worry about my Queen. I know how to take care of her."

"Tell her that!" She pointed at the white Queen standing all alone. "She's the one liable to be crushed in the battle!"

He stared her straight in the eye. "Believe me, my

Queen will come out of this unharmed." The door closed behind him.

China stood in her office, the floor practically trembling as she realized how rocky her world had become. How desperately she needed to reach out and touch something stable! She looked at the phone and knew just whom she had to talk to. She dialed and listened to the distance of a summoning ring, then the metallic announcement, "Parson and Payne, Stockbrokers."

"Arthur Payne, please. This is his daughter calling."

"Hello." Arthur came on the line, his voice a boom of enthusiasm.

The market must be up, China thought. "Hi, Dad," she said with forced brightness.

"China! What a surprise. How are you, sweetheart?"

"I'm fine. And you and Miriam?" China asked after her stepmother.

"She puts up with me," Arthur Payne kidded. His wonderful laugh reverberated, tickling China's nerve endings.

A small silence followed. "Chippy? Something tells me this isn't your once-a-week obligatory call to Father. What's wrong?"

His use of her nickname brought the smart of tears to her eyes. Her father had christened her Chippy when she had been an awkward, gangly teenager with as much resemblance to a piece of fine china as a chip from its rim.

"What's happened, Chippy? Is it your mother? I read about Martin leaving her. Damn Clare," he muttered. "Can I do anything to help?"

Like what? China wondered, and was shocked by how bitter the thought was. "No, Dad," she said softly. "I just wanted to hear your voice."

"Well, if there is anything, you know you can count on me."

But she couldn't, China realized as she hung up. She couldn't count on her father, couldn't trust him to take care of anything for her.

As a twelve-year-old, her parents' divorce had been a bewildering, frightening time. Two years later her father had married Miriam, and there was talk of China living with them for a while. But Clare managed to convince everyone she would *die* of it. China was her only reason for living. Uncontested custody was awarded to Clare in court, and the very next day she remarried. Arthur should have known. He should have fought harder. His and Miriam's home would have been such a wonderful, *stable* home for China.

Instead, she had waded through adolescence with Clare and Milly, a couple of lost souls, as her guides into womanhood. Grief wrapped around her heart as the father she thought she had died and the disappointment of the real man stood in his place. And if she didn't trust him—did she trust anyone? Had she *ever* trusted anyone?

She glanced around her empty office. "My God, this is all I've got."

Five

The esteemed law firm of Hoffer, Kole required an entire floor to accommodate the extensive demands put on its superior reputation. Tongue-and-groove paneling, butter-soft leather furniture, and sound-absorbent carpeting discouraged off-the-street clients. The intimidating interior even caused corporations on retainer to question the validity of the business that brought them here and to regret the damage to their bank accounts.

Escorting an effusive client to the elevator, Reeve sighted China sitting with his secretary. Miracle of miracles, Debra was raptly hanging on every word China said. Scores of international dignitaries had pompously appeared at Debra's desk with not one luring her away from her typewriter or telephone. It was not uncommon to see a man used to attracting attention double-check the lay of his hair or the fit of his suit in the face of her dismissal.

Reeve crossed the open room to greet China and conduct the promised tour. God, but she was beautiful, he thought. An apple-red suit was molded to her endless body, bringing a fresh vibrancy to the stuffy surroundings. Reeve led her first to the law library, hoping to find it empty. As luck would have it, Steve Myers, a clerk, was diligently researching a case for one of the attorneys. It would not do to have the young man witness one of the junior partners making love in the firm's most sacrosanct chamber.

"How did you manage to pierce Debra's steel hide?" Reeve asked China.

She forced her eyes away from the awesome collection of gold-imprinted leather-bound books and glanced over a slim shoulder at Reeve. "Miss Wendell isn't the friendly type?"

"She'd tell the President of the United States to take a seat, then hush him up if he disturbed her with small talk."

"But not Al Pacino," China declared with a sly twinkle. "She's positively wild for the man. Although I'm not the fortunate soul to agent that hot piece of talent, we have attended the same functions. You get a lot of mileage out of what he eats, drinks, and drives."

"I believe you've won my Debra," Reeve complained softly.

"Your Queen Pawn, also, with my Pawn advance." She flashed him a victor's smile as he held the door open for her. They walked a hall lined with solemnly framed diplomas. "I'm impressed," she murmured. The richly carved doors were embossed with bronze lettering and hydraulically hinged to close automatically against felt-padded jambs.

"What are we whispering for?" Reeve wondered aloud.

"Well, just look at this place! I've been in churches and felt less intimidated and less inclined to keep my mouth shut. I feel like God is going to walk out of one of these doors any minute."

A whisper-thump announced the arrival of a third person. "He just did." Reeve then introduced China to Robert Hoffer, a founder of the firm.

On the way out they passed Debra's desk, and she handed China a thick, sealed envelope. "What is this?" China turned it over in her hand.

"Mr. Laughlin's résumé," Debra answered. "I was told to have it ready for you."

China laughed up at Reeve. "You didn't!"

"If I say I will do something, China, consider it done."

She fondled the four corners of the envelope as she sat next to Reeve in a taxi. He directed the cabby to an intersection on New York's south side, then sat back to look at her. Avoiding his steady gaze, she tore at the envelope with a fingernail. Reeve snatched the packet from her hand, stuffing it into a side pocket of her purse.

"You've got all weekend to read it," he said.

She slid a sideways look at him. "Assuming I have no other plans." Her retort was both leading and noncommittal.

His lips formed a hard line, his brow furrowed menacingly. She wanted to remind him that she had every right to do as she pleased, and he had no right to question her, except that a strangely soft emotion in his eyes made her lightheartedly say, "Nothing more interesting than Sunday brunch with Clare, Reeve."

He sat back with a loud sigh that might have been relief, but was probably air in the way of his inflating ego. The relationship was suddenly moving too fast for China. It seemed as if her logic and common sense had always to run to catch up.

They stepped out of the cab on a corner south of Houston, better known as SoHo. Regardless of the fine reputation of some of the small restaurants, China considered it a bit out of the way when they both had offices to return to.

Then, with a flash of insight, she knew where he was taking her. He walked with the proud carriage of a man about to reveal something important. He was taking her to his home! And of all places it was in SoHo! Rationality told her to pull her hand out of his possessive clasp and grab the first cab that passed, but with logic and common sense lost somewhere on Fifth Avenue, she was helpless. Of their own volition her legs stretched wide to keep pace with him. Her eyes searched the lively Art Deco streets, absorbing the sights he saw first thing every morning, the buildings that were his neighborhood. An overlong shaggy haircut and a West Side Russian restaurant had not prepared her for Reeve's living with the bohemians in a converted loft in the SoHo—Cast Iron district, although his driving on the sidewalk should have been a clue.

"Next thing I know, he'll be drinking with his dog," China muttered under her breath as Reeve pulled her into an old warehouse.

"Did you say something, China?" Reeve inquired, knowing full well what she had said.

A ten-feet-by-ten-feet freight elevator yawned open before them. Reeve set the car in motion, and metal gears gnashed together all the way up three floors to his loft.

She let him slide her red jacket down her arms, baring a white silk blouse sheer enough to expose a lacy chemise beneath. Her first thought was that it was warm—for such a large, open area. Warm in temperature and warm in decor. Even as she carefully avoided his eyes she felt him watching her for a reaction.

He chuckled. "You like it. You don't want to like it, but you do."

"Harrumph," she snorted. "I wouldn't put much store

in my taste—I like cold pizza for breakfast too." He shrugged out of his jacket and vest, whipped the tie from around his neck, and unbuttoned enough of his shirt for the collar to flop open. China had never seen him without a jacket hiding his taut-muscled torso. Darts form-fitted his pale blue shirt, and the material hugged the rippling plates of his chest.

"Make yourself comfortable," he suggested. The words disappeared into the huge space. The kitchen was partitioned off, and Reeve ducked in there as China cautiously toured his home.

Contemporary and traditional art in both oil and watercolor filled walls that were either uncovered brick or weathered barn siding carted in from the country. She went farther into the gymnasium-size space. Everything flowed; from a dining area at one end that could comfortably seat eight, to informal seating arranged around a central fireplace, to a working den, then up a three-step platform where a king-size bed was overlaid with a hand-painted spread. A brass fire extinguisher served as a vase for feathery plumes. A wagon wheel had been converted to a chandelier and was suspended on heavy black chains over the fireplace seating group. An antique desk with dozens of cubbyholes was piled high with Reeve's legal briefs. And in front of a long stretch of small-paned windows was a carved chess set, the board a patchwork of ivory and ebony. The chessmen were up to date in simulated warfare with the exception of her most recent elimination of his white Pawn.

That's where he found her when he exited the kitchen carrying a tray heaped with their lunch. He placed the platter on a table in front of the couch and stood up, hitching his thumbs in his belt loops. Following his sweeping gaze, China looked down her legs at her bare feet. She didn't even remember taking her shoes off, yet a quick glance found them, set side-by-side at the door.

She shrugged, feeling silly. "Habit."

"I like it. I like it very much. What else comes off?"

"Your head if you twist the simple fact that my feet are sore."

"Come and eat, China," Reeve ordered with suppressed laughter. "We've got less than an hour before I have to get back to my office."

Fresh rye bread was piled high with smoked ham and Swiss cheese. A bowl of fruit and a dry white wine completed the fare. China curled up on the sofa, her legs folded under her. Her eyes slid over Reeve with fluid contemplation—from his wind-ruffled hair down the strong column of his neck to the wiry black chest hairs curling over the V of his open shirt. What in the world was he doing living in a setting like this? She had figured him for a conservative brownstone like her father's or a conspicuous penthouse with a bird's-eye view of Manhattan. He could let his hair grow another inch and bare *all* of his chest, and he still wouldn't belong in an artist's loft in the midst of offbeat SoHo.

While China picked through her tangled thoughts, Reeve maintained a one-sided conversation, applauding the bakery down the street where he had purchased the bread fresh from the oven and imitating the fussy little butcher who always had a better cut of meat stashed away in the back of his store. He finished lunch and sprawled leisurely on the sofa, his legs stretched out and crossed at the ankle. Hooking one arm behind his neck, he swirled the wine held in his other hand, sunlight chasing the liquid around the bulb of the long-stemmed glass.

Reeve settled quite comfortably into the silence, but the quiet disturbed China. Confronting the stripping, allover gaze of his sapphire eyes was the final devastation. If only she could figure the man out! If only she could stop *wanting* to figure the man out!

"Why do you live here, Reeve?" she asked compulsively. A lazy lowering of his eyelashes and a sardonic smile was all the response she got. "A warehouse loft! Home for a Hoffer, Kole partner? Martin Laughlin's son? He wouldn't have been caught dead south of Houston."

"He was never caught here alive either," Reeve added. The words had a soft quality, the sort that was often called deadly.

"Is that the reason? Is living here insurance that Martin will stay out of your life?"

He rolled forward to set his wineglass down on the coffee table. The movement brought his body angled to hers, the breadth of his chest grazing the tips of her breasts. "It is a welcome benefit. But I live here because I choose to, for the acceptance and sense of belonging. It's like a great big family reunion, complete with wise old grandmothers, wacko once-removed cousins, and brothers you can count on."

He lithely shifted his weight, leveraging her back to a pile of pillows, trapping her under the length of his hard body. Her open hands prevented the crushing contact of his chest. Between the throb of his heartbeat on her soft palm and the silky web his velvet voice wove, her instinct to escape dissolved to hypnotic, rapt attention.

"I live down here for me. My mother died when I was seventeen years old. I have no family to speak of. I took a good look at my life after my divorce and found something missing." His hands framed her face, a thumb rubbing back and forth across her lips. She was aware of only two things—his seductive touch on her lips and his gritty voice in her ear. Her hands casually slid around his waist, her fingers locking together. "I knew I needed contact with people; more than contact, involvement. I get that here. You'd do well to follow my example, China. Look into your own life and find what's missing."

"Why do I get the feeling you believe Reeve Laughlin is what I'm missing in my life?" she said in a husky tone.

His laugh was soft, and the blue eyes that met her gray ones were sparkling with thoughts she couldn't begin to fathom. "It's about time you admitted what we've both known for some time. And you don't just need me in your life—you need me in your bed, in your body."

The bald statement stunned her. A backwash of anger fed her resurging effort to be free of him. "I haven't admitted anything. Get off me! Now!"

He pinned her legs to the sofa and rolled his weight deeper into the soft pocket between her hips. "Honey, we've wanted each other from the first day we met," he drawled. "I do believe it hit me first. There was never any question that I would have you in bed—only how I would get you there and how soon." He settled more comfortably on her, and her body betrayed her by shifting to accommodate him and then melting around him.

"I close my eyes and I can still see you," he whispered at her ear. With a masterful touch he stroked the length of her from shoulder to thigh. "I can tell you what color your shoes were, that your initials were stitched in black on the side of your purse and how many pearls made up your earrings. I knew your breasts would fill my hands and your hips make room for me. And you were tall and long enough for me to look into your eyes and watch you explode as I made love to you."

"Oh, Reeve. . . ." His verbal foreplay made exquisite love to her, as effective at stirring her body as the intimate touch of hands and lips. Even as she held him, felt the ripple of his spine interrupt his sleek back, she begged him to stop. "Don't do this to me, please. . . ."

"Honey, don't fight it." His mouth, insatiably hungry, covered hers, crushing her head deep into the pillows, destroying her resistance. When he pulled away, his breathing was ragged, his words forced from a tight throat. "It hit you too. I saw it go through you like a bolt of lightning. You knew we'd be lovers."

"No, I didn't know . . . I don't know," she insisted. "I'm not about to have a spur-of-the-moment affair with a man I've just met and who is untrustworthy as well. Stop unbuttoning my blouse!"

He froze. His head snapped up and his eyes blazed down at her. 'What do you mean, untrustworthy?"

"Maybe that's the wrong word," China quickly amended. "But you're a paradox, Reeve. And I can't . . . I can't relax with you."

The tense spring in him uncoiled; the weight of him doubled. "Why? Because my office and my home aren't duplicates of each other?"

"In a way yes." He pulled her blouse open. Flames shot through her as his hands covered her breasts, bare beneath the chemise. "Oh. Stop, please. Not with a man I can't trust. . . ." Her aching, taut nipples poked at the satin and lace; fiery tongues licked down her limbs, turning her flesh a rosy hue. Reeve groaned with the delicious pleasure of just being able to touch her.

"Would you like me to move to an apartment?" Reeve asked between nibbles at her flesh. "You can pick it out yourself."

She worked her elbows between them, shoving him away. Surprisingly he let her slide out, rolling back with a groan. "That's even worse," she cried. She moved across the room, inching backward as far as the window wall, the chessboard at her side. "That you live here is unpredictable. . . ."

"For goodness' sakes, China—"

"But that you would move because a woman you've just met doesn't like it is irrational." Nimbly she removed his Queen Pawn and slammed hers in its place, updating the game. "I don't need any more irrational, unpredictable, slap-bang people messing up my life!"

He saved his rebuttal until he stood across the board from her. "Admit you've fantasized us in bed together."

"I'll admit nothing of the sort."

"You disappoint me, China. Either you're deluding yourself, or that's an outright lie. Whichever it is, I didn't expect it from you."

"Okay, I admit it," she hissed, immediately chagrined that he had goaded her to it. "So what? It doesn't mean I will make love with you today." He moved his Knight to her King Bishop, gloating over his victory.

China's eyes grew wide with fury. "It doesn't mean I will go to bed with you in the future either." She attacked his Queen by advancing her Pawn on his Bishop.

Instead of getting defensive, Reeve smiled. China reconsidered the board and saw how self-defeating her last move was.

"Now we're getting somewhere," Reeve said, advancing his Queen. The full attack had begun.

"Don't count on it. A friendly roll in the hay maybe; getting into my life, no!" Her Knight to his Queen Bishop. "God only knows how many more quirks you've got up your sleeve."

The verbal volley flew across the table, the furious clip of wood against wood punctuating each rejoinder as the game moved from contemplative combat to all-out warfare. By the time China realized how Reeve had manipulated her into making reactive plays instead of sticking to her original game plan, it was too late.

Palms pressed to the table edge, they glared over the wooden soldiers. "I will mate you, China," Reeve boasted with such arrogance, she could only see red instead of the encroaching checkmate he was warning her of.

"I told you when we met that I like being unattached—no meals or midnights. Remember?" She followed his sapphire eyes to where he had dropped them to his Queen. He had only to advance her to win.

"We've already been together at midnight and this is

our second meal. And like it or not, China, you are no longer unattached."

She'd lost! Or was about to.

She stood straight, facing his smug expression without flinching. Oh, wouldn't she love to wipe it off his face! Well, if he was going to win—he was going to earn it. With her gray gaze centered on his features she calmly unbuttoned first one cuff then the other of her already gaping blouse.

"What are you doing, China?" He narrowed a skeptical glare on her.

"If I'm to be mated, Reeve, I intend to enjoy it to the fullest." She turned around and walked up the steps to his bed.

Six

Reeve chuckled. The sound was benevolent and grated on China's nerves, as if she were a precocious youngster to be humored. Even as she let her blouse float from her fingertips, even as the afternoon sun pearled her bare, sloped shoulders, Reeve indulged her with a quiet laugh. The clear guileless stare she gave him brought the sound to an abrupt halt.

"I don't know what you're scheming, China," Reeve growled, beginning to feel the first unsettling quake of shaky ground. "You're not the type to just give up and lie down."

"Give up, Reeve?" She flicked open the button of her skirtband and ran the short zipper down. A twist of satisfaction buffered some of her anger when uncertainty clouded his face. "I didn't give up. You won fair and square. This is what we were playing for, isn't it? The right to mate me? To take me to bed?"

He approached her, hesitated, took a few more steps,

then stopped. He shoved his hands into his trouser pockets and glared at her. His head was slightly bowed down, his eyes the blue of an overcast sky as he studied her. Her skirt dropped to the floor and he gnashed his teeth together. He wanted her and he couldn't have her! Reeve told himself.

Every inch of her long graceful legs were exposed with her flat stomach and round bottom sheathed in a provocative panty-slip. She flicked a satin strap from her shoulder to hang loose on her arm. Reeve wondered just how far she would go with this dare. How far would he let her go? Who will back down first?

China raised a black silky brow at him, questioning his reticence. "Oh, I'll admit I was naive; I thought we were just playing a chess game at first. But I catch on fast. Come on, Reeve. You don't think I'm going to let you mate me on the board until you've literally earned it." She flicked the other strap down, and the lace border of her chemise slipped to rest on the prominent peaks of her breasts, two dark slivers of her dusky nipples exposed over the top. "I may even decide that it won't merit the final move when it's over."

His footsteps shook the floor as he angrily closed the distance. "Put your clothes back on," he softly commanded. He bent to pick up her skirt and glared into her eyes as he held it out. Her irises were dark smoke, her emotions hidden behind those foggy screens. "Here, put this on."

She plucked it from his fingers and dropped it back to the floor. "What's wrong, Reeve? You don't want your prize? There is an old saying—'Be careful what you wish for, you might get it.' "

"I'll get it all right," he snapped. But he had already tasted the honeyed promise of her. He would not settle for a fast bitter mouthful now. Snatching her blouse up, he gingerly replaced her straps and started dressing her.

"I'll get what I want. And it won't be some rushed affair with you lying passive, taking it like it was a punishment." He awkwardly worked the soft material up her uncooperative arms, then moved around to the front of her to button the blouse. "Dammit, China, I don't understand you."

"Hurrah for me," China drawled. "That, I think, would earn me a move. Alas, there isn't one left to save me."

He tossed her skirt into her open hands and turned his back on her, stomping down the steps.

"Are you throwing the game, Reeve?" Her eyes were big and wondering.

"Damn the game," he bellowed. The sweeping arc of his arm scattered the wooden pieces all over the room. "The hell with the damn game."

China stepped into her skirt, tucked in her blouse, and whipped up the zipper. "Game called due to heavy casualties on both sides," she lamented, surveying their soldiers lying all over the room. And there in the middle of the otherwise empty board, counter to the laws of probability, stood his white Queen.

"Well, well," China drawled. "Look who survived. You did say not to worry about her. Sure enough, she came through even *your* destructive behavior."

He stood at the window staring out, the muscle along his profiled jaw clenching as he gnawed on his anger, tasting the sharp bite of regret. "Are you ready to leave?" he asked, quietly prodding her along.

She walked to the door and slipped into her shoes. He put on his tie, vest, and jacket. They were polite and reserved. He ushered her out the door and into the freight elevator, and their silence continued for the entire cab ride.

When the taxi veered to the curb in front of her building, Reeve leaned across her to flip up the door release. "I'll pick you up at eight-thirty tomorrow night."

"Reeve, I'm not going to see you again."

China sighed as his arm curved around her, preventing her from stepping out onto the street. She gazed at the buildings, the people, everywhere but at him.

"You'll see me," he insisted.

"The game is over, Reeve."

"Right. Now we'll get down to serious business."

China crawled out of the cab, then looked in the open window of the back door. "I won't be there if you come."

His compelling features, so photogenic and clearly cut, resembled cold granite. She ran into the building as the cab pulled away.

Self-deception was not one of China's weaknesses. As brutally as she looked past hypocrisy or duplicity in others, she was just as honest about searching for her own motivations. Standing at her office window, she had finally had to sit down as shock at her behavior and relief at its outcome started her knees quivering like soft-set Jell-O.

What could she have been thinking of? Stripping in his loft! Daring him to get in bed with her! What if he had? And at the time she had thoroughly believed that he would. Considering herself fortunate that he had put an end to her unbelievable lunacy did no good. The truth was, she deeply regretted even that. She wanted very much to make love with Reeve. And she had nearly accomplished the deed in a manner so full of self-deception, it made her sick.

Damn the man! He didn't belong in her life. She didn't want him in her life.

A note from Marce lay on her desk: Vince Charles of the Charles Place Ad Agency wanted to meet with her. Perfect. In a matter of minutes China had made a dinner appointment with him—for Friday night at eight.

Going directly to the restaurant from the office safe-guarded her from any possibility that Reeve would second-guess her intentions and arrive early. At pre-cisely eight-thirty China believed she could hear the echo of his fist on her door. Rolling a mouthful of salad over her tongue, China could only remember, with vivid clarity, the personal taste of a sandpaper-velvet tongue.

Arriving home she checked the door for signs that he had been there, a note, something. There was nothing. In her dark apartment she played back her answering machine to see if he had called. He hadn't.

From the side pocket of her purse Reeve's résumé taunted her. Unfolding the two typed sheets, China read the dry, factual data. Brooklyn-born. Harvard-educated. Golden boy in the district attorney's office—that would qualify him to defend Clare on a murder rap. Shortly after joining Hoffer, Kole, he was involved in a prec-edent-setting trial against the Internal Revenue Ser-vice. Because of Reeve's expertise, the little guy won. Instant junior partner. He hadn't climbed the rungs of the professional ladder, he had flown to success on an express elevator.

China felt as if she understood him better, respected him a lot more. She didn't feel closer to him. He wasn't inside a résumé. She held the papers to her face think-ing, maybe. But he had never touched them; they just smelled like paper.

She thought he would call on Saturday. He had said something about a weekend conference—but still, she thought he might at least try. Nothing with Reeve would be casual, and both of them were already onetime losers at serious relationships. And when she felt herself weak-ening in her resolve not to see him, she had only to turn to the society page and a nasty, gossipy commentary that was a direct result of Reeve's article two days ago.

Damn him! He had done this to her. Would do it again, no doubt.

Making an endless list of errands, China left her apartment early in the morning and stayed away all day.

That night she played back her telephone messages twice—listening for someone who might have hung up.

It was midafternoon Sunday when China let herself into her apartment after an utterly bizarre brunch with Clare. She glanced at the phone as she passed it, commanding her legs to continue to the bedroom. She threw on old jeans and a red T-shirt bleached pink, her standard apartment-cleaning outfit. She made the bed, scrubbed down the tub, squirted glass cleaner on the windows and tables, then finally broke down and activated the answering machine.

Three phone calls from Paul Doran. At least someone wanted to speak to her.

She was cleaning the oven, protected to her elbows in clumsy rubber gloves, the fumes of the cleaning agent stinging her eyes. The doorbell rang and her heart leaped into her throat. She took a deep, hopeful breath before calling out, "Who is it?"

"It's Paul, China. Why haven't you called me?"

"Come on in, Paul. I don't think I locked it."

She heard the door open and shut and looked up from where she was kneeling on the floor to meet with Paul's scowling face. "Are you crazy? Not locking your door? God, you're a mess. Why didn't you call me back?"

"It's nice to see you, too, Paul," China said sweetly.

He had the decency to look embarrassed. He also looked his doctor-best. His medium brown hair was conservatively cut and styled; nary a hair would disgruntle an intolerant hospital-board member. His long lean face was shaved, and his cologne drifted with tangy appeal through the oven-cleaner fumes. His deep brown eyes were not, however, smiling.

"Here, catch." China tossed up the aerosol container and Paul automatically caught it before shrinking away from the bright yellow can, horrified.

"What do you think you're doing?" he barked, slapping the can on the countertop. "You don't throw something like that into the hands of a doctor. It's got stuff like acid and lye in it."

China stood up from the hard floor, rubbing her sore knees. "I didn't realize that psychiatrists had to protect their hands. Or have you become a surgeon since I last saw you?"

She handed him a clean, damp cloth and he washed nonexistent chemicals from his hands. "Look, China, are we still on for tonight? Is it formal? What time should I pick you up?"

"Yes. Film openings are always formal. Six-thirty for cocktails." Every six months or so, Paul and China got together. It was a friendly divorce, the least China deserved after the hostile marriage.

"Great," Paul said. He tossed the rag in the sink on his way to the door. "See you at six-thirty. Don't be late."

She was just securing the clasp of her pearl choker when Paul rang the bell. Black tie was perfect on him. He stood in the doorway and let out a low wolf whistle. His brown eyes widened as he took in the breathtaking picture she made in an off-the-shoulder, full-skirted gown of emerald green, iridescent taffeta. Her raven hair was pulled into a braided chignon and emphasizing her graceful throat adorned with strands of pearls. She rustled with every step and left a cloud of perfume in her wake when she went to the closet to get her wrap.

Stepping out into the hall, China was suddenly spun around by Paul's abrupt hand on her arm. "You're not going in those shoes, are you?"

It was not a question but a demand to change them. Barefoot, she and Paul were the same height; in her evening shoes she was a good bit taller. "I'm sorry, Paul, but these are the lowest heels I have. My last pair of flat shoes wore out, and I'm afraid I haven't bought another pair."

"I won't go out with a woman who is taller than I am." He used to say she'd be perfect if only she weren't so tall. By the time they got divorced, the "if only" list had grown to insurmountable proportions; most of them as impossible to change as her height.

"Fine, I'll go alone."

"You must have another pair of shoes!"

"No, I don't." China was beginning to think going to the theater without Paul was a great idea. The evening was taking on all the strain and tension of the last year of their marriage.

With each passing hour China regretted not following her instinct. Had Paul always been so petty and picky? He didn't have a nice word to say about anyone. By the time they sat side by side in the cab going home, she was relieved to have the evening over. "No, don't bother to see me upstairs," she suggested politely, sensing a new unpleasantness in Paul and wanting only to get away from him.

"Of course, I will," Paul said, paying the cabby. "You never know who might be waiting in the hallways. It's late and dark. I'll see you upstairs."

Paul snatched the key from her fingers and unlocked her door. He walked in ahead of her, turning on the lights and looking in all the rooms. "Good night, Paul," China said coldly. "And I'd rather we didn't see each other again. I don't think you enjoyed tonight any more than I did."

"China," he murmured. The caress in his voice crawled up her spine and rang a three-alarm bell in her head. "I've missed you, China. There aren't any like you. Tonight . . . tonight, all I could think of was getting you back here . . . alone."

She tried to twist free of his encircling arm. "Don't, Paul. Go home now and don't call me again."

He backed her against the wall, and instead of panic China had the stupid urge to laugh. He kissed her as his arms went around her. "This is childish, Paul. I *don't* want you to stay. I *don't* want you to kiss me. And I *don't* want to fight with you."

"It was always so good with you." Now she was frightened. "Not for you though. I was stupid and selfish. But I'll make it up to you . . . tonight. It will be so good."

"You're right." China pushed at his chest to no avail. "You never thought of anyone but yourself. I never mattered. It was always when you wanted and over when you were finished."

He cut off her words with another urgent kiss and China fought in earnest to free herself. "Let go of me, Paul—"

"You heard the lady," a deep voice said from the doorway.

Paul froze and China cried with relief. "Reeve! Oh, Reeve."

Paul took a half pace back but he kept his arm around China. His brown eyes slid dubiously to the man in the doorway. The blue blaze of Reeve's glare centered on that offending arm, and Paul sensed the danger of leaving it there. China slid along the wall putting a breathing space between her and Paul.

"Who are you?" Paul asked. The huffy sulk in his voice set Reeve's teeth to gnashing.

"The lady wants you to leave," Reeve ground out. "I suggest you do so. Now!" The smile that curled Reeve's lips was bitterly cold; it would have made a sensible man run for his life.

China stared at Reeve, grateful that he had come when he had, thrilled that he had come at all. She didn't notice his shabby clothes or the unkempt hair or the torn tennis shoes. Only his wonderful face.

"China, who is this man?" Paul demanded.

"The white Knight," she whispered through her smile.

"Come to save the Queen," Reeve added, bowing slightly.

"His name is Reeve Laughlin."

"Laughlin? Laughlin? Oh, yeah! Your old man took my old man's place with Clare," Paul said, relaxing to a slouch.

"You were invited to leave, Doctor Doran," Reeve reiterated in a tone that was deceptively silky.

Paul looked a bit bewildered. Then his glance whipped to China's bemused expression, and everything became very clear indeed. "Oh-ho! You've been giving it to China in my place as well."

Reeve's fist snapped out so fast that Paul had already hit the opposite wall and rebounded before China could even shrink away. "Go now, Doctor Doran," Reeve warned. "While you still can."

Paul rubbed his jaw, sidling along the wall as far away from Reeve as he could get. His churlish voice when he reached the haven of the hallway was sickeningly sullen. "What are you trying to do, China? Sleep in your mother's bed? Another stepbrother? Jeez, you need a psychiatrist."

"She had one," Reeve snapped. "He was lousy."

Reeve's foot kicked the door shut with a slam, and China started to laugh. Even she could hear how shrill the laugh was growing, and her arms came around her body to hold back the hysteria. Reeve drew her to him, and she leaned on the solid protection of his chest, her head falling to his shoulder.

"You're safe now," Reeve crooned and she nodded.

"You have anything strong to drink? Whiskey or brandy?"

"In the kitchen, over the sink."

He walked her to the living room and settled her on the couch before leaving her to get a brandy for each of them. When he came back, she was pacing the room, working her nerves off. "I'm okay now, Reeve. I'm not going to collapse."

"Drink this," he ordered.

"Why did you come?" she asked, turning her eyes on him.

"We have unfinished business and I don't talk to answering machines."

A sunburst broke throughout her body and sent streams of gold rushing along her veins. "You called me? Did you?"

"I tried." He set his glass down and stood back to look at her. "Was a queen ever more beautiful? You look too perfect to touch."

For the first time she noticed that he was wearing old patched jeans and a sweatshirt that was paint-spattered and torn at the seams. His tennis shoes had probably never seen a washing machine, and his hair looked as if it hadn't been combed with anything finer than his fingers.

She unclasped her pearl choker and dropped it on a table. Next she plucked the pins that held her braid in a tight coil and shook her hair loose. It sprang free in an inky waterfall, thickly mussed and softly curved from the molding twist.

"I'll do the rest," Reeve said. He pulled her to his hard length, his fingers finding the gown's zipper tab.

She leaned back as far as the embrace would allow. "The rest of what?"

"The rest of the undressing." The hiss of her zipper

being let down proved his intentions. "I told you, we have unfinished business."

The crush of their embrace was all that held the dress in place as his mouth covered her parted lips. She opened her mouth, hungry, meeting his urgent demand with ferocious need. This is insanity, her mind screamed. But it's such rapturous madness. She shoved his sweatshirt up, massaging and kneading his taut flesh, shuddering and moaning when his fingers traced every small knob of her spine. He swallowed every sweet liquid sound she let slip into his mouth.

"I want you on a big, soft bed, China. Take me there."

If he hadn't said anything . . . if he had just pulled her down to the floor. But his explicit request required her to think. Resisting the pull of the sensual whirlwind, she stepped back, a flattened hand holding her dress in place, and sank into a chair. The blood pounded in her head with such slamming force, she had to concentrate to decipher the arguments rocketing about her brain.

"This is all going too far, too fast," she breathed. "I don't want to make another mistake, Reeve."

"Then don't send me away. That's the only mistake you can make." The silk-cloaked words were a sensual rasp. She tipped her head, and Reeve gazed down at the billowing emerald cloud of her gown. Her luminous gray eyes were large pools of silver in milk-white skin.

"Why did you come here tonight?" she whispered, aching for the truth.

"To touch you. To make love to you." He heard the sigh that parted her lips, felt her skeptical inspection of his attire. "It was a very sudden decision."

She nodded. "Yes, sudden."

"And inevitable. And oh, so right."

She wet her lips, his eyes watching every flick of her tongue. "How long did you . . . were you at the door?"

"Long enough."

"Tell me, Reeve," she cried. "Tell me what you heard."

He crouched on his heels in front of her. "I heard enough to know you've needed a man like me for a long time." His gentle touch traced her collarbone and burned a path to the hollow between her breasts where his subtle fingertips created an ache under her skin. Her hand, pressed to the dress front, curled into a claw, to hold on to her senses as much as her gown.

He worked his fingers into that numbing grip, lifting it away. "Let me see what I've envisioned a thousand times," he murmured. The folds of the gown's bodice were turned down with the same soft rustle of tissue paper taken from a present. He groaned as his eyes drank in the sight of her upturned breasts, swollen with her arousal. He leaned forward and softly kissed the dark peak of first one, then the other.

"My God, you're beautiful." His voice was smoky, as heated as the blue flames that flared in his eyes as he watched his own big hands mold the shape of her breasts. China stared at his face, breathless at the powerful effect she had on him.

Inevitable. She kissed him, a brush of her lips across his. And oh, so right. She needed this man.

He gathered her up in his arms and carried her across the white carpet to the bedroom. He kissed her with fierce possession once more before setting her down on her feet. The gown fell to the floor with a muted rustle. She took his outstretched hand and stepped over the voluminous mound of material.

Surrendering to a blind passion, China melted to him, floating in the intense world of heightened perceptions. She relaxed even as her muscles drew taut with arousal. He touched every inch of her as he carefully removed the last thin barriers of stockings and panties. When she stood naked before him, he lifted her up and laid her in the center of the snow-white bedspread. Her hair was a velvet fan of liquid ebony and her skin awakened to a heated flush.

He stripped impatiently, never taking his eyes off her long-legged beauty. She gazed through a haze of desire at every virile inch of him. "You're magnificent," she whispered.

He moved over her, putting his warm palms to her cheeks. "So you said once before." His tongue traced her earlobe, igniting sparks of exquisite pleasure-pain that sped along her nerves. "Said I could sell anything to a woman." He chuckled, the low growl tickling her ear. "I had a hell of a time selling myself to you."

"You shouldn't be here," she murmured, kissing and licking the skin of his shoulder, loving the special taste of him, driving him to madness. "I'm going to hate myself in the morning."

He buried his lips in her hair, his voice a torn, ragged shred of its former strength. "You're going to love yourself in the morning. In less time than that."

His hands preceded his lips, one stirring to life, the next feeding on the fruits. His teeth nipped the sensitive cord in her neck, counted the ribs to her hips, moistened the soft flesh inside her thigh. Licking fire up to her breasts, he sipped at the sweet, dark nipples until China arched like a bowstring pulled to lethal tension. The clamoring need to envelop him in the softest folds of her body consumed her.

"Slow down, babe," Reeve crooned. "Not so fast."

"But I need you," China pleaded. "I need you *now.*"

"You're running a marathon at sprinting speed." He slowed the rhythm of her pulse with long soothing strokes. "Slow down, you're missing too much."

"But—"

"Afraid I'll leave you behind? No, babe. You're coming with me."

He rolled to his side, watching her body respond

under his hands. She turned her head into the bend of his elbow, nibbling at the drugging male skin.

"Touch me, China." Pressing his thumb into the tender spot in her wrist, Reeve slid her hand from the mat of chest hair. Guiding, he moved her hand over the plates of his chest, the tapering of his waist, the sharp jut of his hipbones, leading her long, graceful fingers until she gave him a pleasure that rocked his hard body.

"China, oh, China. . . ."

"Oh, Reeve," she moaned. "Please, Reeve. Please . . ."

He moved over her, separating her legs with his knee. Her head was thrown back all the way, her eyelids so tightly squeezed together, her lashes might have been tied in knots. She gnawed on her bottom lip with white, hungry teeth.

"Open your eyes, China," Reeve commanded, lowering himself down upon her. "Look at me. Look at us."

Her eyes flew open, and Reeve gazed down into a wild, primitive need he had never seen before. And clear, as clear as looking into a spring pond and counting the shimmering pebbles at the bottom.

"Come with me, babe," Reeve raggedly demanded. They were locked together in timeless union. At his words fear stabbed her, the flat of her hands pressed his chest away, even as her fingers curled into the wiry black hair between the masculine nipples, pulling him closer.

"Sh, sh." Reeve sought her amazed gaze. "I won't leave you behind. As long as it takes, I'm here. . . . I'm staying."

She wrapped her arms around his neck, intending to pull him down to her. But the arch of his spine was implacably rigid, and she was drawn up to him, clinging desperately.

Clutching a fistful of her silky hair, Reeve pulled her

head back a few inches. "Open your eyes, China. Watch us."

And what she saw was a man's face washed with passion, boyish and young with discovery. Her eyes met his, gray eyes locked with blue, splintering to silver and sapphire as the first explosion shook through them, then the next . . . and another. When she screamed his name, it was swallowed up by his open mouth. Thirstily he drank every drop of her honeyed passion as it seeped out of her, moan after small moan.

Seven

The primitive and wild strength of their passion stunned China. Just thinking of the sweet giving and satisfied taking sent off thrilling little rockets deep inside her. Reeve moved to her side, intimately gathering her to his hard leanness. Instead of getting up and pulling the covers back, he grabbed at the quilted spread, drawing the ends over them, unwilling to break the spell he had begun weaving the moment he arrived. Now they lay knotted together in tender harmony, enveloped in warmth and drugging body scents.

Reeve pushed wayward strands of hair from her face and faintly brushed her swollen lips with his thumb. China's eyes flickered over his face, taking in his expressive mouth, the strong cut of his jaw, the glorious fringe of thick black lashes. His eyes were smiling, the blue deeper and darker than she had ever seen it.

Thirty years of emotional self-control had been blown to bits, but then she had never been subjected to so potent an attack before. She expected a flood of shame for her unrestrained behavior, not this warm radiation suffusing her whole body. As Reeve had promised, she loved herself. Loved her leadened muscles so tensed moments ago. Loved the languorous world she was floating in. Behind the smile in Reeve's eyes, the wonder of her lingered, and she knew that even he had been slammed to earth like never before.

She laughed softly. "You certainly know how to make a woman love being a woman."

"You've heard the old saying about no such thing as a frigid woman—just inconsiderate men."

"Frigid. No, I never felt frigid. Incompetent sometimes, inadequate all the time."

"You are none of those, babe." His arm went under her shoulders, his legs intricately twined with hers. "You are a queen and I am your besotted subject." There wasn't even a tremble of delight left in China.

Her bruised lips were ultrasensitive to his long, soothing kiss. The harsh rasp of their breathing eased from sharp sucks and explosive gasps to deep, even sighs.

China fell asleep and Reeve turned back the corner of the quilt to gaze at her by moonlight one last time before he, too, gave in to bone-deep exhaustion.

China woke as the first fingers of dawn scratched pearly light into the dark room. She was alone in bed, and it was the muted sound of Reeve moving around the end of the bed that had stirred her. When he crouched to find his clothes, China reached over and lost her fingers in his velvet black hair.

"Don't go," she whispered.

He raised his face up to her and kissed her quickly. "Don't tempt me. I've got an early court date and I can't stand before the judge in the rags I wore here."

"Just for a little while?"

His eyes slid to the illuminated clock on her bedtable;

it read six-thirty. "No time. But your request for an encore is much appreciated."

"It isn't an encore I want," she teased. "I want the whole performance repeated, start to finish. I'd give you a standing ovation if I had the energy to stand."

"A rave review will do." He pulled his jeans on and sat back on his haunches again, gazing at her face.

Poking an arm further out of her quilted cocoon, she ran a fingertip over his carved features.

"Such a hard face," she whispered.

"Comes from removing my beard with hammer and chisel."

". . . for such an easy man." She giggled.

"Easy, huh?" Even though he was scowling, there were smile lines at his eyes. "I suppose I should be grateful you didn't say soft."

His hand curved to her neck, the warmth coursing desire through her veins. The pressure of his mouth on her lips swelled the regret of his nearing departure.

"I've got a nightmare week," he said, backing away from her and the temptation that would make him late. "Debra couldn't free a single night for me."

"Likely story," China tossed off. But her heart twisted with fear. Instinct told her he wasn't the one-night-stand type, but instinct had failed her in the past.

"Don't look at me like that, China. I plan to have a long run at this house." He sat on the bed to tie his shoes. The mattress gave under his weight, rolling China toward him, and she curled her sleep-warm body around his waist.

"Reeve, did you come Friday night?"

"Of course not—you weren't here."

China popped up on her elbow. "You did come! How else would you have known I wasn't here?"

"If you'd been here, you'd know whether I'd come or not."

She fell back on the bed, smiling with utter contentment as he walked out the door. She had a lover! A magnificent, considerate lover! It was such a perfect solution, she didn't know why she hadn't thought of it before. Just because she wouldn't marry again didn't mean she had to be celibate. She was a mature adult with needs and desires, and every right to have them satisfied. Besides, discreet affairs didn't lead to wrenching divorces.

"I don't believe it!" Marce exclaimed, following China into her office.

China raised her eyebrows with mock indignation. "I'm only twenty minutes late, Marce. It might be a first, but it's not a crime."

"I'm talking about your dress." Marce ogled the simple, sophisticated style of her employer's cream and tan print. "It's the first time in three years you haven't worn one of your suits of armor."

"*Armor!* Messrs. Klein and Givenchy would hang themselves by their tape measures if they heard you say that."

"Forgive me. Elegant and chic suits of armor they were. Better?" Marce rolled her eyes expressively.

China wondered at Marce's observation. She *did* feel less vulnerable, secure in some intangible safety zone that allowed her to strip away her mental shields. How in the world could an affair with a man who seemed to threaten her on all fronts make her feel indestructible?

China chuckled. It was unexplainable but it felt great. Then she saw the two-page spread laid open on her desk. Bubbling laughter died on her lips as she flipped the slick pages over to see the cover. "*Faces* magazine?" she cried in a voice strangled by disbelief and horror.

With utter amazement she glanced over at Marce. "Do

you know how many favors it costs me to get one of my clients in this damn magazine and now *I'm* in it when I don't *want* to be?" The star attraction of the photo spread was Clare, profiled over the last thirty-eight years with each of her five husbands. China had never seen them all lined up that way. And they'd even dredged up a fuzzy old picture of her grandfather, Lester Howard. And Joey—she touched the small military school snapshot, realizing how much she missed him. It was as close to a family album as China had ever seen.

After scanning the captions, she read the copy—one long quote from Reeve strongly suggesting that Martin had fallen victim to foul play and ending with a real tear-jerking plea for anyone with information. . . . Damn him! And *his* picture didn't appear anywhere!

"China?" Marce queried softly.

"I'm fine. Really, I'm just dandy." Yet she clutched the collar of her dress, aware of how very thin the material was.

"If you say so. Anything special we should take care of before you tackle the new batch of contracts that just came up from legal?"

Contracts again. She should have stayed in bed this morning. "As a matter of fact, there is something." Mischievous lights danced in her wide eyes. "Who's that kid over at *Variety*? You know, the one who's so grateful that we've been sending him out as an extra? Get him on the phone for me. I want to get a bogus 'rave' review planted in Wednesday's edition." Let's see how *you* like it, Mr. Reeve Laughlin!

Thursday morning, before leaving her office to oversee an important audition, China circled in red ink the review she had dictated over the phone and had it sent to Reeve's office by special messenger. At ten o'clock that night she heard his distinctive knock at her door.

"Hi," she whispered, opening it and drinking in the sight of him.

"Hi," he murmured back. Into her hands he placed a tall vase made of emerald-green ceramic and stuffed with bright red paper poppies.

"What's this?"

"Life colors. You know, the green of a thriving forest, the red of a beating heart. If ever a place needed some life, this one does."

"A poet too," she marveled, pretending to pen that fact down in an imaginary notebook. He smiled, and she was struck by how tired he looked. "Hungry?"

"Starving." Then, finally, he kissed her, each of them savoring every second to make up for the four-day separation. Tearing his mouth away, he said, "Do you suppose I could have a sandwich before the dessert?"

"Sure." She stepped back, noticing the *Variety* tucked under his arm. She raised a querulous eyebrow at him, waiting for his reaction.

"Lady, you gave me a hell of a lot of adjectives to live up to here, not to mention adverbs." Fatigue deepened the crevices that captured his mouth; the lambent lights in his eyes were dimmer than usual. Maybe that's why he wasn't as angry as she had expected.

"All you star performers are insecure deep down," she observed dryly. "However, it's said that precurtain jitters make for a better performance."

"How did you manage it?"

"Oh, I have connections too." Plucking her copy of *Faces* from the weekly mail, she slapped it into his hands. "Certainly mine aren't as *illustrious* as yours!"

"Now, China, I didn't promise."

No, she told herself, because he *kept* his promises And he wasn't able, or willing, to make concessions for her. He wanted her to change, to mold her to his way of thinking, to cut herself off if it hurt. China moved off to the kitchen, a cool smile hiding her pain. What did it matter? He was her lover, not her husband. He's temporary; you make allowances. Right?

Reeve lounged in the doorway as China piled the ingredients for his sandwich on the counter. When he began quoting from the review, China ground her teeth together. " 'Reeve Laughlin gave a *superior* rendition,' " he read out loud, and hot blood stained her cheeks. "And I love this part here—'A closing climax that *blazes* with passion.' "

China spun around and stamped her foot. "Damn you! You're supposed to be mortified—"

"Are you kidding? Over"—he searched for another phrase to read—" 'a delicious, dramatic portrayal'?"

"Stripped naked in public. Don't you feel betrayed? Your privacy has been invaded!"

He laughed uproariously as he crossed the room, and China wanted to cry with frustration. His arms closed around her waist, and he lifted her off the floor, walking out of the kitchen, raining kisses on her face and neck as she tried to keep his sandwich balanced on the plate.

"What did you want to do, China?" he asked between kisses. "Give me a taste of my own medicine?" He strode across the living room as she squirmed to be free. "I do have one objection," he complained, setting her back down. She glared up at him, raising her chin defiantly. "You put me under 'New Acts.' Honey, I'm a pro."

China cried out and socked his arm. "Eat," she ordered, and at his seductive lift of one brow she snapped, "Your sandwich."

He ate half the sandwich and fell asleep on her sofa in midsentence. For a long time she stared at the vase and flowers, so vibrant in the snowy room. Life colors and a compelling man in her living room. How unexpected!

And she did feel alive. Her nerves prickled under her skin whenever Reeve was near, her heart slammed at her breast, seeking the answering throb in his chest whenever she was in his arms.

It had been a long time—three years to be exact—since she had let any real emotions move her. She looked around at all the white contrasting with the bright bouquet and Reeve's coppery flesh. A cool, sterile environment where she had put her deepest desires on ice. That's what her apartment was. A refrigerator!

She quietly crept across the room to Reeve and crawled between his warm body and the sofa back. These were the moments she lived for, and they increasingly outweighed the price she paid. He had steadily, progressively, infiltrated her defenses. She melted to his shape, lulled to sleep by the soothing throb of his heartbeat on her cheek.

In the darkest hours of the night she woke to a pair of hands pushing her sweater up, a pair of warm lips catching one taut, eager nipple as Reeve used his teeth delicately.

"Feed me, China. I'm so hungry for you."

"Oh . . ." The moan slid softly from her lips as Reeve filled all her empty spaces.

Eight

Thump, thump, thump. China groaned and rolled over in bed. Burying her head under a pillow, she cursed whatever idiot was banging on her door at such an ungodly hour. She was just sliding back down into the nowhere of sleep when it came again. Thump, thump, thump.

She crawled out from beneath her warm quilt and pushed her arms into her robe, indifferent to whether it was inside out or upside down. Blindly groping along the walls, she shuffled to the door. With a bleary eye to the peephole she saw Reeve, cheeks hollowed and lips puckered. "Whistling, yet," she muttered. She slid back the bolt, unchained the door, and opened it.

"Good morning, China!" He sailed right past her and into the apartment. "You're not still in bed on this sunny morning! It's a super Saturday! Get dressed and let's get out into that sunshine. It won't be long before winter drives us all inside."

Her weary body followed the door as it closed, until she was resting against it. "It's barely seven o'clock," she croaked. The sharp male scent of his after-shave worked on her senses like a jolt of smelling salts. The border of his Irish knit sweater met the pockets of muscle-defining gray wool slacks, making China that much more aware of her rumpled state.

He put his hands on her hips, pulling her to his broad chest. "You smell good in the morning." He buried his nose in her hair. She squirmed out of his sinewy arms. "Gorgeous to look at too."

"Uh-huh." Her eyes were thin slits as she looked down at her cold feet peeking out from the hem of a lopsidedly belted robe. Her face was puffy and without makeup, and her hair was sleep-snarled. "Go home," she mumbled. "Come back in an hour."

"Get dressed, honey. We're going out for breakfast, then to an auction at Sotheby's. Afterwards . . ." He put his finger to his chin, pretending great thought upon their itinerary.

"Afterward?" she asked suspiciously.

"We'll play it by ear. We've got all day."

"Great, then you can come back in *two* hours," China said over a yawn.

"I missed seeing you yesterday. Late night?"

"Mmm-hmm. But award dinners always run three hours over. What did you do?"

His wide smile turned suddenly stern. "I was lectured on the proper behavior for a Hoffer, Kole partner. Special emphasis was put on keeping my 'blazing passions' and 'dramatic climaxes' private in the future."

"Hoffer and Kole read *Variety*?" China laughed.

"I doubt it. Most likely a client brought it to their attention."

"You mean, they don't know about you? Why, Reeve Laughlin, you've been passing yourself off as a typically conservative Hoffer, Kole attorney! And now they've found you out!"

Serves him right! That damn *Faces* article had dogged her, all night. You'd have thought Clare was some addlebrained imbecile who had lost Martin on a busy street corner, for all the jokes China had had to listen to.

"Come on, China, get ready," Reeve prodded. "I'll wait for you here."

There was little point in arguing, China decided. Like it or not, they were going out. He'd plant his feet in one place till he took root, if that's what it took to get his way. Besides, she was beginning to wake up. She padded off to her bathroom knowing that a stinging shower would clear the last cobwebs from her brain.

Reeve waited in the living room, considering its subtle transformation since the first night he had been here. On the glass table sat the brilliant green vase stuffed with scarlet poppies. China had added plush green throw pillows to the ice-white sofa, and flourishing ivy plants hung in all the windows. He had penetrated the battle line and was welcome in the enemy camp.

She called out from the bedroom, pulling his attention back to the present. "What was that?" he called. "Couldn't hear you."

She stuck her head out the door. Her hair dripped beads of water from the shower and her arms hugged a drenched towel to her breasts. "I said, what do you want me to wear?" she repeated.

"Blue. You always look fantastic in blue."

She rolled her eyes heavenward. "I mean, where are we going? Is it cold out? Will we be inside? Outside?"

"That's what you asked? I could have sworn you asked what I wanted you to wear."

She growled with playful despair and flung the soggy towel across the room at him. Then she slammed the door shut. But not before Reeve caught a glimpse of long, slim legs, invitingly curved hips, and blood-stirring, dusky nipples.

She was startled by the door opening behind her and spun around to see Reeve sauntering into her bedroom. She opened her mouth to protest as her eyes dropped to his hands, which were nimbly unbuckling his belt. Her smoky, anticipating gaze lifted slowly to his face as her mouth closed and her lips curved seductively.

"Like I said," Reeve drawled. "Breakfast first."

They met each other with passionate intensity, tumbled to her mussed bed with gleeful enthusiasm, and made love with boundless joy.

The sheets were twisted around their hips. China held his strong hand out in front of her, playing her fingers in and out of his. Rolling over, she rested her chin on his chest. He had to look over the high crest of his cheekbones to see her.

"Do you ever think about having children, Reeve?" The question just popped out of her mouth, seemingly without forethought. Reeve froze beneath her, his muscled chest as hard as cement. China's gaze bounced away from the icy chips in his eyes.

"China . . . are you . . . ?"

"No!" She sat up, naked to the waist, the soft pastel sheets draped around her hips. "No, I was curious, that's all. Didn't you and Ann ever plan a family?" Why didn't she drop the subject? It was obviously not one Reeve wanted to discuss. Yet China found herself holding her breath and feeling as if she were precariously balanced on the edge of a precipice.

Reeve relaxed fractionally to learn she wasn't pregnant. Lightly tracing the luscious curves of her breasts, he gave more attention to each discovery of his fingertips than he did to her question. China flinched away from his touch so that he lifted his fingers from her sensitive skin to comb them through the tangled silk of her hair. "Kids need two parents and the security of a stable home. I think Ann and I both knew from the first we wouldn't last long." A strange pain threaded his voice, a pain China suspected was born long before he'd even met Ann.

"Didn't you have a secure home, Reeve, before your mother died?"

"No. Oh, my parents weren't divorced, although it might have been better for all of us if they had been. I'd have known what to expect from each of them then. As it was, Martin took off whenever a new woman interested him. When the novelty wore off, he'd come back home. For a while I'd have a father again, just like all the other kids . . . until the next time."

China rested her chin on her knee, her thoughts sliding back to the past. "Paul and I never planned kids either. Never even talked about it."

"You see. Your heart told you he wasn't the one." Reeve lifted her chin from her knee, the pinch of his finger and thumb turning her face to him harsh enough to bruise. "What's this all about, China?"

She shrugged, honestly unsure. "Aren't we abnormal? Isn't it human nature to want to leave something of yourself behind after you're gone? A new generation to carry on?" The heaviness in her heart seemed a direct result of their recent lovemaking. Instead of her usual purring satisfaction after the sweet joining of their bodies, a throb of illusive longing was still hammering within her. Making love should make life, China thought, if two people were meant for each other.

"It might also be human nature not to inflict suffering on an innocent child," Reeve countered bitterly. "You and I both know how temporary relationships are. I wouldn't wish any child, let alone one of my own, into a home with two people who will eventually go separate ways. No kid should have his loyalties torn in two."

"You're right," she whispered shakily. Pulling herself together, she gave Reeve a broad grin that hurt her inside. "I guess I just wondered if you had some macho need to see a little boy with your face carrying on the family name. Most men do, and you are the last Laughlin, after all."

"But I'm not most men."

China bounced off the bed, pretending the subject no longer interested her. Maybe if they'd met each other first . . . if they hadn't come to each other disillusioned. But because they'd been losers at love, they both had painful knowledge of how it would end. When the silence stretched an unnatural length of time she looked over her shoulder to Reeve. Her sudden jump from the bed had pulled the sheets away, exposing every magnificent inch of his bronzed body. He seemed unaware of his sprawled nudity as he stared out the window.

"A little boy with my face?" His eyes narrowed as if he were trying to conjure up the little tyke. "There'd have to be someone I was very sure of and something inside promising this time it's forever."

And, China knew, they weren't forever. And Reeve didn't make promises he couldn't keep.

He turned from the window to watch quietly as she got dressed. If China had had a medieval suit of armor in her closet, she'd have put it on. Instead, she dressed for the climate of a crisp autumn day in white wool slacks, a heaven-blue blouse with white piping and a navy and white cable-knit sweater. Pulling her hair back from her temples, she secured the raven silk with white porcelain combs set behind her ears, leaving the rest to spill down her back.

"Let's go," she urged as Reeve finished dressing. Her enthusiasm felt forced, even though she needed to be exhaustingly busy. Anything not to look inside and face her own emptiness.

Midafternoon found them wandering Reeve's neighborhood streets under the golden sun of an Indian summer day. They had pretty much worked their way across town. Breakfast at a hotel was followed by an hour at Sotheby Parke Bernet, where they watched without making a purchase. A stroll down Fifth Avenue, a midtown lunch, and then SoHo.

Reeve whisked her up and down the streets, introducing her to his adopted family: the butcher who saved his best cuts of meat in the back for Reeve; the baker's wife who made China smell her tortes and pies and went into paroxysms of ecstasy over her own cheese cake; the leftover hippie who made throwaway dresses out of the Sunday comics encased in plastic wrap. Reeve didn't just want her to meet them—he wanted her to love them. It eased some of the morning's misery. He was offering her all he had; it wasn't his fault that it wasn't as much as she wanted.

Arms full of purchases, she followed Reeve to the freight elevator of his building. She had known all day they would end up here. It was nearly five o'clock, and they had plans to make dinner together.

The massive elevator door was just sliding closed when a voice called out, "Reeve. Hey, Reeve. I look for you all day." The words were so thickly wrapped in an Italian accent, they were barely understandable.

Reeve drew the door back, and China saw an elderly man in work clothes hustling toward them, waving a fistful of papers.

"Luigi!" Reeve called out in surprise. "China, this is Luigi Mancuso. He has a leather repair shop around the corner. Luigi, China Payne."

But the man was too agitated to do much more than nod in China's direction. His attention was on the papers, and he kept trying to press them into Reeve's hand. "What it means? Eh?"

The very legal-looking packet was unfolded and China could see that it was a summons to appear in court.

"You're being sued, Luigi." Reeve read, skimming the legal language. "By your cousin Salvatore Adamo."

"The bastard!" Luigi screeched. "I should know, eh? You put a knife in a man's hand, he stab you in the back." Luigi was clearly upset. "Come, Reeve, I show you. I got proof. Eh, you help me."

The older man latched onto Reeve's arm and was trying to pull him out of the elevator. "Wait, wait, Luigi. Today? China and I were on our way upstairs to have dinner. And what's this talk of proof?"

Luigi's eyes grew large and his face turned beet-red with suppressed fury. "What proof, you ask! Come, I show you. We can't wait, my friend. The paper say I go to court Monday."

China saw that Reeve's loyalties were torn between their own plans and helping the old man, so she stepped forward to see if she couldn't relieve the situation. "Reeve, go on with Mr. Mancuso if he needs you. I can start dinner and we'll eat when you get back."

The gratitude in Luigi's eyes made the small sacrifice worthwhile. Reeve searched his hip pockets and came up with a key ring. China took it and Luigi Mancuso bowed repeatedly in gratitude.

She let herself into the loft and rushed to the dining room table to drop her heavy bundles. Rubbing sore arms, she ran back to retrieve the other parcels Reeve had set on the floor. Closing the door, she glanced around the large room. Other than a rumpled bed and Reeve's morning coffee cup on the fireside table, the place was in spick-and-span order. Surprising, China thought, considering that he didn't have a woman to take care of him, assuming he didn't—no, she was not going to get possessive!

She was itching to open his desk drawers and clothes closet to find out more about him, but instead, she rummaged through his kitchen cabinets for the spices she needed to make spaghetti sauce. Laying everything out on the counters, China collected what she would need from their purchases and cleared the rest of the packages to an out-of-the-way spot. She flipped through Reeve's record collection and put on a Luciano Pavarotti album.

Delicious scents were bubbling from the pans and filled the loft. Cherry logs lay on the fireplace grate ready with kindling, so China balled up the morning paper, shoved it under the kindling, and fanned the fire to life. Then she rushed up the three steps to the bed and started pulling the sheets up.

She flapped the sheet in the air and the enticing scent of Reeve washed over her from the covers. It was such an exhilarating sensation that she pressed her face into his pillow and took a great drinking breath of him. She knew she was behaving like a teenager bowled over by first love, but even adults could be adolescent when they were alone, she told herself. Drunk on the scent of Reeve and feeling more than a little giddy, she made the bed, chastising herself for behaving as if she were playing house.

What a clash of contradictions he was, China thought. Begrudging his own stepmother one hour of paid, professional time, yet eagerly rushing off to the aid of a needy old man on a Saturday afternoon. Another idiosyncrasy to add to the long list.

Luciano was singing away, and China's heart seemed to fly with the soaring notes. The only other thing out of place was the area around Reeve's chessboard. The chair was angled away from the table as if someone had just left it. An ashtray on the windowsill spilled over with cigarettes smoked to the filter, and a glass of yesterday's bourbon sat on the floor near the chair's legs.

She had seen Reeve smoke only two cigarettes in two weeks. Yet a whole pack of twenty lay stubbed out in the glass ashtray with the twisted, empty pack next to it. She looked down at the game board, wondering why he had obviously spent so much time here. His white Queen still stood in the center of the board. Only, now she was protectively circled by her eight Pawns. Reeve had put away the rest of the scattered pieces.

She stretched out her hand to clear the board, but couldn't force herself to put the Queen in the velvet box. Getting superstitious, China? she chided. Afraid you'll suffocate? Ridiculous! She and the Queen were not one and the same; it had been a game, and the game was over. She left the game board as it was and pushed the chair up to the table. Gathering up the glass and ashtray, she carried them to the kitchen where she put on a pot of water to boil for the pasta.

When Reeve let himself into the loft, Luciano was celebrating life on the airwaves with garlic and oregano wafting along. Reeve called out to China from the doorway: "Is that spaghetti I smell?"

"You want proof?" she exclaimed with a sincere try at an Italian accent. "Come, my friend, I show you."

He joined her in the kitchen. After the cold outside he was grateful for the heat of the fire and the oven and the warmth of the woman. "Hello, my friend," he growled in a voice he never used with Luigi. He laced his arms around her waist as she spread garlic butter over thick-crusted bread before popping it under the broiler. He pressed his face into her hair, taking deep gulping breaths.

"You smell good enough to eat," Reeve muttered hungrily. "Mmm, like tomatoes, onions, garlic. . . ."

His hands were pulling her blouse free of her waistband, and China slapped them down. "Put the pasta in the water, will you? Add a tablespoon of oil so it doesn't stick."

With one arm hugging her to his body, he poured some oil and dumped the spaghetti into the water. "There. Now, where was I?"

"Ruining dinner," China scolded. He turned her around in his arms and his lips covered hers just as she opened her mouth to argue. Her sounds of protest slowly turned to little moans of pleasure and, when the buzzer for the garlic bread went off, to muffled screeches of panic.

She wedged her elbows between them and dragged her mouth free of his plundering tongue. "Stop, Reeve. Dinner is burning."

"So am I," he groaned, pushing his hands up under her blouse.

"But I'm hungry."

"So am I."

Between his hands fumbling with the clasp on her bra and his mouth shooting flames down her limbs, China considered putting the whole dinner on hold. Then the ringing of the telephone joined the insistent buzz of the timer.

"I give up," Reeve complained. He moved to the telephone, and China saved the garlic bread from the oven.

"Hello," Reeve snapped before the receiver was anywhere near his mouth. His blue eyes shot daggers at China as she failed to bite back a smug laugh.

A voice could be heard coming through the line, speaking very fast and very loud.

"Calm down, Sal," Reeve said. Then, cupping his hand over the phone, he said to China, "Salvatore

Adamo." China moved her mouth into a small O of understanding.

"Yes, I know, Sal," Reeve conducted his conversation while China began putting dinner on the table. "I spoke with Luigi just a short time ago. . . . No, no, I'm not representing him. You're taking him to small claims court, you don't need a lawyer there."

Reeve paused while more excited language came from the phone. "Yes, Sal. Next time you sue Luigi, I'll advise *you*."

"Next time?" China exclaimed as Reeve took the seat across from her. "They do this often?"

"About once a year." Reeve laughed. "They are cousins operating separate businesses in the same building. They're supposed to split the overhead—utility bills, taxes—straight down the middle. They fight it out in court every time their fiscal year ends."

"And stay together anyway?"

"Oh, they like it this way. I doubt they could live without it." He poured the Chianti they had bought that afternoon. China sipped it, smiling over the rim of her glass at him.

"I'll bet you don't charge them either."

"For what? When you get right down to it, they know more about small claims court than I do." He tasted everything. "It's delicious," he pronounced. "I don't know why, but I wouldn't have thought you had such culinary skills. Didn't you grow up with a cook in residence?"

"No, Clare never could keep help," China replied. She had wondered how long it would be before one of them brought up Clare or Martin. "Clare fires everyone after three days."

"Except Milly."

"Oh, she fires Milly too. Milly just won't leave." She

narrowed her eyes, thoughtfully immersed in the past.
"I cooked because Clare couldn't and Milly wouldn't."

"What do they do now?"

"Flip a coin. Heads they eat out, tails they order in."

"Have you always taken care of her?" Reeve asked.

"Yes, I guess I have, at least since Dad left." China
tipped her head. "You'd like my dad. He's remarried, and
Miriam is as good as they come."

"A stepmother too."

"Yes, a stepmother too."

They took the last of the wine to the hearth and Reeve
put another log on the fire. Luciano had finished his last
breathless aria and neither of them bothered to move
the needle back to the beginning. For a while the snap
and hiss of the fresh log licked by the flames was the
only sound in the loft.

China sat on the floor, resting her back on a large pillow propped against the sofa. Reeve lay flat out on the
fur rug, his head resting in her lap. China asked how it
was with Martin and played with the thick lock of hair
that had fallen across his forehead while he talked.

"I never took care of Martin, just the women he left
behind—penniless and crying. I swore I'd never be tangled up with another until Clare."

"Why is she different?" China asked.

"Two reasons." Reeve rolled his head on her lap so that
she was compelled to look down into his eyes. "She is his
wife. And she is your mother."

He came up on his elbow, his face just below hers. "I
wanted to see you again." A light butterfly kiss that
barely brushed her mouth sent her heart tumbling
through her rib cage. "And again." Exploring lips swept
her cheek until his teeth softly sank into her earlobe.
"And again."

Reluctantly he drew away, his eyes probing her features for a response. But speaking of Clare and Martin

had invited them into the room, and it was as good a time as any to get some questions out of the way. As if reading her thoughts, Reeve moved away, poking at the fire and waiting.

"Any trace of Martin?" she asked.

"Traces, yes. Martin, no." He hunched in front of the fire, glancing over his shoulder at her. The reflection of the red flames cast a demonic glare over his sharply planed face. "It won't be long though. I think he wants to be found. He's traveling under his own name, writing checks for hotel rooms, even using his charge cards once in a while. And he stays a good week in each place."

"What does that mean?"

"It means he moved out of his last hotel Friday just before the private investigator got there. Sometime next week a check or charge card receipt will reach the bank, and we'll know where he is."

"Next week," China breathed.

The wistful sigh of that single phrase drew Reeve's mouth into a tight line. "Why did you say that like it was a deadline—one you'd like to see postponed?"

How well he understood every nuance of her voice. "It is, I guess." She raised uncertain eyes up to him. "We can't really be sure what Clare will do when you bring him back. She may still decide to drag him through a very nasty, very public court fight. She may really want to divorce him."

"They can't hurt you, China."

"You can say that. I don't have your anonymous walls to hide behind."

He stood and walked past her. She heard the sigh of the sofa cushions accept his weight. China had expected, hoped, he would come back to her. Bereft of the human contact, she wrapped her arms around her knees and drew them up to her chin.

"China." His solemn voice broke the heavy silence. His

blue eyes ran over her, and she instinctively drew her knees tighter to her chest. "Come live with me, China. I'll share my fortress with you."

She stared at him. "No." She didn't even bother to think the matter over. "I have a home."

"That isn't a home. It's a couple of rooms where nobody lives . . . not even China Payne." He rolled forward until his arms were resting on his knees. "I want you here with me. I need to know that when I turn over in the middle of the night, you'll be there beside me."

The visual picture he drew in her mind made her mouth dry. It could be lovely—for a while. But if she were going to live with someone, she might as well make the supreme mistake of marrying him. Not that Reeve had asked her, but her personal commitment would eventually be as complete, and when it ended, the loss as devastating.

"Wants and needs aren't enough," she said finally.

"And you don't think there's more between us than that?"

"Good sex."

She hadn't meant to make him angry with her flip retort. But rage flared in his eyes, and his mouth compressed as if he had to bite down on his anger to keep from spitting it out.

"Not love?" he growled.

"Gratitude, maybe, for sexual satisfaction. But I'm not fool enough to mistake that for love."

"Could you be fool enough to mistake love for gratitude?"

What did he want from her? China wondered. To say she was in love with him? If they were still playing chess, such an admission might earn him a move. What game was he playing now? "I've been in love, I know what it is."

"With Paul? Do you really believe you were in love with him?"

"Yes, I was in love with him. And if I ever doubted it, I found out how much when I walked into my own home and found another woman taking care of my husband. If you judge love by how deep the knife blade sinks, I was very much in love with him."

"Will you tell me about it now?"

"Nothing to tell. I saw all the warning signs and chose to ignore them. Until he made it impossible." Tears sprang up behind her eyelids, and she blinked them away, determined not to feel anything, just to relate the facts. "I was away for a few days. Joey and I went down to Disney World. I came home, walked into the apartment, and came face-to-face with his latest. Wearing my satin robe, standing in my kitchen, making Paul a cup of coffee with my percolator. He was still in bed, damp with the sweat of their lovemaking."

"I'm sorry, babe." Reeve spoke tenderly.

"Yes, me too. She knew her way around my home very well. Obviously it wasn't her first visit."

Everything she said hit close to home. How well Reeve remembered his mother, staring in a mirror when she didn't know Reeve was watching. How she would touch each imagined wrinkle, looking for reasons why the man she loved didn't love her in return. The way she would stare at Martin's plate on the dinner table, slowly withdrawing into her quiet hell as she made excuses to Reeve that his father was working late. "Why did you stick it out for so long?"

"I know better what I *don't* want in my life than what I do want. I don't want five husbands . . . I don't even want two. I married for life, or thought I had. I wanted to make it work because I vowed not to look back on a life littered with ex-husbands."

"Why do you still see him?"

"I don't very often." China took a deep cleansing breath, discovering that a great weight had been eased off her chest. "I'm not so different from you. Everyone needs family, and that's what he is. Mine consists of my ex-husband, half brother, and stepmother; you've got a butcher, a baker and a plastic-dress maker. You take what you can get."

He chuckled when she twisted the nursery rhyme, then said something totally unexpected. "You're the only woman I've ever brought here."

China wanted desperately to reclaim the mood that had surrounded them at dinner. Easy, sensuous, and noncommittal.

"I still won't move in with you."

He nodded, not looking terribly disappointed. "Will you compromise?"

The side of his mouth kicked into a grin, and China felt a dare coming. "You want us to go to a hotel halfway between your place and mine?"

"Stay till tomorrow night."

She looked around at the warm room, the crackling fire, the golden lights. "Yes, but only till tomorrow night." He sighed and fell against the cushions, throwing his locked fists behind his head. She narrowed her gaze at him. "Why do I get the feeling that's all you wanted in the first place? . . . Reeve, did you trick me into this?"

Snapping laughter sparked sapphire lights in his eyes even though he tried to keep his features expressionless.

"You did," China shrieked. Then she laughed, appreciating the success of his ploy. "What would you have done if I'd accepted the first proposal? Huh?"

"Shoved my socks over to make room for your nylons."

She couldn't tell if he meant it or not.

"Do it for me again, China. What you did the first time you were here."

She raised her eyebrows in question.

"Take your clothes off. One piece at a time. But slower, much slower, while I watch." His eyes burned over her skin across the five feet that were separating them. "I won't stop you this time."

Nine

China walked into the subtle amber glow of the firelight. Her clear gaze locked with Reeve's as her fingers disappeared under the silky fabric of her blouse and smoothly unfastened the waistband of her wool slacks. Her eyes never strayed from his as her palms skimmed the pants over her hips to the curve of her thighs. Bending forward, she lifted one foot out of the soft wool and then the other. Her thick, heavy hair fell over her shoulders, the weight of it loosening the porcelain combs.

Slipping the combs out, she dropped them to the table with a clatter, then neatly folded her slacks and draped them over the armrest of a nearby chair. She felt Reeve's avid gaze lap up the stretch of her long, nylon-sheathed legs to the dip of the shirttails hiding her flat stomach and rounded bottom.

His lean, compact frame was as silently still as a poised panther while she teased him with the slow production of undoing each button of the pale blue blouse.

China could feel the tension coiling in him, radiating from him, until the air around them crackled with the electricity of the moment. A muscle jumped along his jawline as the second button was released and the fabric responded to the strain of her breasts by separating to expose the shadowy valley between them. Open to the waistline, only one button to go. Reeve's eyes grew intensely blue. A sigh parted his lips, and China loved the spell her slow unveiling cast upon him.

The blouse floated to the floor from the tips of her fingers, landing to the sound of him sucking air between his teeth. A groan accompanied his expelled breath.

"You're sure you don't want to help me?" she asked in a whisper. Huskier than usual, her voice was laden with womanly invitation.

He smiled, a slow spread of his chiseled lips, then settled himself deeper into the plush cushions. "You're doing fine all by yourself, babe."

She eased the elastic band of her panty hose over her bottom before perching on the armrest of the chair where her slacks lay. Gradually the sheer nylon was peeled down her legs and, as was her habit, she gently massaged her freed toes. Reeve knew he was watching a nightly ritual; her every action was so uninhibited, so personal.

"Which next?" she asked, standing to her full height, barely covered in a provocative lace bra and matching bikini panties.

"Like I said, you're doing fine on your own."

He made it easy and delicious. What woman didn't fantasize doing a striptease in sensual, private surroundings with one spellbound man her audience? She released the front catch on her bra, and the interlocking parts plumped open, the filmy lace still wrapped around the full flesh it was meant to support. She peeled the material away from first one breast then the other, as one might gently take the thin skin from a grape, exposing the ripe fruit. Staring at his face, she saw an unsuppressible urgency claim his features. He stood up in one rolling motion and agilely pulled off his creamy sweater. The firelight played over his bronze corded muscles as he walked toward her.

She shook her head, swirling black silk hair about her shoulders. "No, you had your chance to play a part in this fantasy. You'll wait now." She stepped away, keeping more than an arm's length between them.

"China? . . . Babe? . . ."

"Stay there, Reeve," she warned with an extended finger. "I'm not done."

She walked around the coffee table and he began to pivot on his heel to keep her in view. "No, Reeve, stay where you are."

Coming up behind him, she feathered her fingers over his back, relishing the bunch of muscles reacting to her touch with a tense contraction. Reaching her arms around his waist, she unbuckled his belt. When his hands moved to help her, she captured his wrists and put them back at his sides.

Pressing her full length against him, China let her hands wander across his chest, brushing masculine nipples to arousal, curling her fingers in richly matted chest hairs. He groaned as he reached behind him for her hips, his fingers sinking into her flesh.

"Uh-uh. Don't touch," she cautioned, moving his hands back to his sides.

"You're torturing me, China," he ground out.

"I know," she whispered, tasting his flesh, leaving a damp trail as her tongue moved over him. "Nice, isn't it?"

Kissing and nibbling the stretch of his spine, China slipped her lace panties off and held them out in front of him before dropping them to the floor. Next her fingers sought the catch on his slacks and loosened them, crushing her breasts to his back.

When each masculine article of clothing had joined its female counterpart on the floor, Reeve lost the tenuous hold on his self-control. He spun on his heels and bent to pick her up. China was amazed that he could lift her so easily, walk with her, and not strain to breathe. She was no small package to cart around, yet she felt dainty and feminine by the very ease with which he carried her across the long room. Her body curled in his arms as he went up the three steps. He threw back the painted spread and gently laid her on the bed.

"You've driven me wild, China," he admonished, coming down beside her. "I don't like to be pushed to such a frenzy that I'm not able to linger over the loving." His mouth devoured hers with a rush of need, pushing her head deep into the mattress.

Working her mouth free, China wanted to regain the sense of power with which this whole seduction had begun. The sudden, unexpected shove of her arms flipped him to his back so that she lay sprawled across his length, and Reeve was now prisoner to her voracious appetite.

She controlled the pace, offering him the pleasures of her body as she tested new skills and acted out deep fantasies. As she tantalized him with a rain of kisses she held her head, lost his fingers in her silken hair. His wiry leg hairs tickled her bare breasts and Reeve kneaded her tender shoulders until she thought he would leave bruises on her pale skin. Her softness melted to his hardness; silk to steel in magical unity.

Reeve swept his hands down her body, the friction of his palms rasping over her nerve endings. He kissed her with quickening nips on her shoulders, at the curve of her waist, behind her knees. And he kissed her with an intimate thoroughness that had China pressing her fist to her mouth to muffle her cries.

"Now, babe," he commanded, as she gently raked her fingernails down his sides and over his hips. "It's got to be now."

Without warning, and with a strength that amazed her, Reeve lifted her up and united them. Her senses teetered on a heaven-high cliff; then she began that thrilling fall through space and time. *Not yet.* China wanted the pleasure of caressing to go on and on but they were both past the point of controlling their bodies with their minds.

This time Reeve didn't have to tell her to open her eyes. She gazed with awestruck wonder at the throbbing passion she provoked in this man. The depth of what she had unleashed in him heightened her own arousal until it exploded and splintered throughout her.

Caught in the maelstrom, she gasped for air, then was pulled under the drowning waves and gave in to the whirling sensation. They clung together as the storm of passion receded to calm. They floated on lethargy, as warm as if the sun were beating down on them from a summer sky.

Reeve rolled her to his side and China gazed around the cozy loft. His gentle fingers played over her, drawing her close. Lit by the fire, all his possessions took on the patina of an old photo. The brass pieces reflected the hearth flames, condensed in their surfaces. The wood floors were burnished amber as fiery tongues danced over the ceiling. Her skimming gaze fell on the chessboard and the white Queen surrounded by her soldier Pawns. How lovely and comforting it looked, flushed by the fire—like a miniature fortress reflecting distant campfires as all the loyal subjects guarded their royal charge.

China had never felt more protected than she did at this moment with Reeve wrapped as solidly around her as the Pawns around their Queen.

"Wake up, China." A man's deep voice began to register through the layer of cotton wrapped around her brain. She knew Reeve was calling, but she wasn't sure if it was a dream or real. Her head refused to budge from the pillow.

Then big hands shook her, bounced her on the mattress; China had the irritating sensation of being dumped around inside a padded washing machine. When she opened her eyes, Reeve was bent over her, his features barely discernible in the pale moonlight. He was dressed and holding a robe out for her. "Come on, China. Get up."

"What's wrong?" She sat up, pushing tangled hair out of her face. She knew by the throbbing ache in her head she had only been asleep an hour or two. "Why do I have to get up?"

"Don't ask questions. Just put this on." Reeve slid her arms into the robe, and his around her waist to lift her out of bed, that warm bed that her body yearned to fall back onto. The lining of the garment was silky cold against her sleep-warm skin, and China shivered as Reeve belted her up and led her across the room.

"Reeve, wait! Where are you taking me? It's the middle of the night!" She looked for signs of fire or flood, some catastrophe that would make him drag her from a deep sleep, force her into a cold robe, and push her out the door without even letting her put her shoes on.

He was wearing frayed and shabby clothes resembling those he'd worn the night he had come to her apartment to make love to her. A cold draft ripped a little more sleep from China's brain, and she realized that she was in the elevator, and the elevator was going down. Her feet were cold, her hair was wildly uncombed, and she wasn't wearing a robe but a trench coat. A man's trench coat!

The elevator opened in the basement garage, and China saw Reeve's burgundy Porsche parked a few feet away. She huddled against the back wall of the elevator shaking her head. "Oh, no. I don't move until you tell me where you're taking me. *I'm naked under this damn coat, for heaven's sake!*"

"You'll be fine. No one's going to see you."

"Right. 'Cause I'm not going anywhere."

"Okay, we'll do this the hard way."

He didn't cradle her in his arms this time; he simply threw her over his shoulder like a sack of grain and walked to the Porsche. China kicked her legs and pummeled his back with her fists. She might as well have walked to the car herself for all the good her struggling did her.

"Reeve, please, please, at least let me get dressed. *Please.*"

"Seeing as you're giving me the option of saying yes or no, I'll say no."

"Then I demand it!"

"Still no."

He made her crawl over the driver's seat to the passenger side so that she couldn't escape while he was rounding the car. He manacled her wrist with his fingers to prevent her from jumping out the door until they were far enough from the loft that she wouldn't dare leave the car in her condition.

"I know. You're one of those men with a fetish for driving around on public streets with women nude beneath their trench coats."

He only smiled at her, his laughter rumbling around in his chest. Whatever he was doing, he was having a great time doing it.

He drove like a crazy man, wildly tearing down the streets so that China's biggest fear became an accident. How the hell would she explain what she was doing on a cold October night, in a speeding sports car, with nothing on under her coat?

He pulled up to the curb and cut the motor. "Come with me."

"Oh, no. I stay right here." China looked out her window and saw they were parked in front of the high-rise building where the Hoffer, Kole offices were located. When Reeve climbed out of the driver's side to come to her door, she pounced on the lock to keep him from opening it. Where the hell did he think she was going to go in a man's trench coat and no shoes? The grate of his key invading the lock scraped at her nerves, and China knew she was helpless to resist him.

Dumped over his shoulder once again, China begged him to put her down. "I'll walk, okay? Just put me down." He set her on the ground and she glared up at him. "I'm going to hate you for this. Honest to God, I hate you already."

Reeve rattled the building's locked front doors until the night watchman came to open them. China couldn't meet the guard's eyes as he peered out, his hand resting on a holstered gun.

"Why, it's Mr. Laughlin," the guard exclaimed. China hid behind Reeve's broad body as he slipped inside the lobby.

"I need to get in my office, Albert."

The guard had turned his back on them. He walked across the marble-floored lobby and sat down at his desk. Reeve's request had him scratching his head through a sparse thatch of salt-and-pepper hair and peering up skeptically. For the first time he took particular notice of China. She dropped her head and stared at the floor. A furious blush burned her cheeks as she felt the guard looking at her wild tangle of hair and the oversize trench coat. Thank goodness he couldn't see her bare feet from where he sat!

"I don't know, sir. I mean, you can go up certainly; just sign in. But . . . well, I'd have to know who the young lady—uh—is."

"This is my sister, China." China swallowed her shocked gasp just in time. His sister! How could he say that after the passionate hours they'd spent together? "I'll need her services. She knows shorthand. Had to get her out of bed."

"Your sister, you say?" Albert wasn't buying it. "I don't know. . . ."

"Look, Albert"—Reeve dropped his tone to a conspiratorial whisper—"I just got a call from the police station. An important client, a prominent public figure . . . he's—he's gotten himself into a bit of trouble. Embarrassing trouble. The kind that's got to be kept out of the papers. I have to get the man out of jail and I can't unless I get up to my office. China can read my secretary's shorthand."

China narrowed her glare on Reeve. It was possible, she supposed. Maybe he *had* gotten a call. He had barely been able to rouse her; the phone might have rung and she hadn't heard it. But why did she have to be here? She didn't know shorthand at all!

"Important man, you say?" Albert was turning the sign-in book around for Reeve's signature.

"Very. Important to the firm also."

Albert wasn't about to be the cause of trouble between Hoffer, Kole and an important client.

Reeve finished signing his name and grabbed China's hand to lead her to the elevator bank. She didn't dare turn around to see if the guard was watching. He wasn't going to believe a word of this once he saw her bare feet.

China yanked her hand from Reeve's once the elevator doors closed. She turned into the corner, her arms crossed at her breasts, and her back to Reeve. His strong hands turned her around, and he pressed his body to hers and traced her angry features with his finger. China closed her eyes and kept her arms folded.

When the doors crept open on the darkened Hoffer, Kole offices, China tried to stand her ground. Reeve didn't even ask her to budge, he just bent down and caught her behind the knees and shoulder and carried her through the lobby, down a long hall and kicked open a set of double-hung doors. Moonlight poured in through the uncurtained windows, glittering on the gold lettering of the books that lined the other three walls of the law library.

Reeve stood in the middle of the room, slowly pivoting with China in his arms, his face tipped up and his eyes canvassing the numberless shelves of bound volumes.

"I've always wanted to make love in this room."

"What?" China rolled her head to the curve of his shoulder with a groan. "Is that what this is all about?"

He set her down on the thick brown carpet and unbelted her trench coat. Shoving the buff coat off her shoulders, his eyes raked over her flesh that was already beginning to glisten with the sheen of decadent desire.

"Every time I come into this room with its tomblike hush and see the sober faces bent over mile-thick tomes searching for a precedent, I think, what this place needs is a good passionate scream."

"Why didn't you tell me! I could have gotten dressed first."

"You wouldn't have come." He gathered her soft nakedness to the rough scratch of his clothes, then pressed her down to the plush carpet. "Making love in the law library isn't logical, practical or acceptable. Why, it's probably sacrilegious."

He was right on all counts but one: She'd have come.

Dawn was breaking in pink-and-yellow ribbons by the time they let themselves into the loft. They fell into bed with barely enough energy to scoot the few inches to cuddle up. It was well past lunchtime when they breakfasted in bed. Croissant crumbs and the sheafs of the Sunday papers spread in disarray finally forced them to get up and start the day. When China stepped into the shower to plunge her head under the steamy spray, she wasn't surprised to open her eyes and find Reeve stepping in with her.

"Is there a water shortage?" China gazed through water-spiked lashes, already anticipating his big hands soaped and gliding over her.

"Small hot-water tank," he lamented, working a cake of soap into a creamy lather.

His slick hands swept her ivory curves, so reducing her insides to jelly that she braced herself with hands spread on the chocolate tile walls to either side of her. Circling her waist, Reeve moved against her, gliding smoothly, lathering his chest from the suds on her skin.

"That's some technique," she purred. "What do you call it?"

"Saving soap."

"Another limited supply, hmm?"

"Turn around. I'll wash your hair." She closed her eyes and tipped her head back, loving the feel of his powerful hands working over her scalp.

She tried to do the same for him, but when she stretched her arms to pour the shampoo, he caught her breasts in his palms. Suddenly her hands were falling to his shoulders and clasping him close to her.

China chose one of Reeve's powder-blue shirts to wear, not wanting to spend another whole day in the only outfit she had with her. Indian summer had ended abruptly, and the first winter winds were whistling outside the loft. Curled up in a deep chair with an afghan draped over her bare legs, China thumbed through a cookbook looking for something inspiring to make for dinner.

Reeve lay stretched out on the sofa, watching a Sunday-afternoon football game. Every now and then he jumped up and coached along with the stadium crowd. Most of the time he just lay there, a can of cold beer resting on his taut belly, a bowl of nuts within reach. It was probably the most normal few hours they had ever spent together.

The letdown began as she finally put her clothes back on. China regretted leaving the loft as she would an island paradise. They had carved a special, private world out of these two days.

"You're awfully quiet," Reeve said, sitting beside her in the Porsche. Taking her hand from her lap, he squeezed it warmly. "Want to change your mind?"

She lay back on the butter-soft leather and turned her head to look at him. "About what?"

"Living with me? We can pack your bags when we get to your apartment."

"I have a confession to make," China bantered dryly. "While you were shaving I looked through your dresser drawers. You don't have room for my things. . . . Your socks have already been shoved over to make room for your sweaters."

Was that relief that allowed him to drop his lashes over lazy eyes? Disappointment that pulled the ends of his mouth down? She couldn't—wouldn't—live with him. Having given him her passion, she feared he was stealing her heart.

On the other side of her door the phone was ringing. As Reeve slid her key into the lock it stopped. He followed her over the threshold and into the kitchen. She tossed her purse on the counter, her keys into a glass bowl, and activated her answering machine with an automatic fingerflick that said she did this every time she came home. When Milly's voice filled the small kitchen, Reeve saw China come to a standstill. A thread of desperation in the aged, reedy voice on the tape brought China spinning around on her heels.

"Miss China, come quick. Whatever time it is. You gotta stop 'em. Quick, Miss China!"

Ten

The answering machine clicked off, and China continued staring at the instrument. "Them? Stop them? Clare and who? *Who?*"

"Let's go," Reeve ordered.

But China kept staring, unable to believe her ears. Reeve saw those silvery lids close over her eyes and her toe set to tapping with the staccato rhythm of a news bulletin coming over the wire services. "No, no"—how calm she sounded—"I think I should call Milly and see what this is all about."

Reeve grabbed China's purse from the counter and dug her keys out of the bowl. "Does Milly do this often? Call and leave messages like that?"

China shook her head. "Never. Well, almost never."

"Then let's stop wasting time and do as she asked."

"Oh, no," she drawled. There'd been enough embarrassment the first time she'd gone with Reeve to her mother's. And China couldn't afford to let shame and resentment build up to such levels that it came between her and Clare. Reeve would go his way one day, but China had a lifetime to get through with her mother. "*I'm* going to my mother's. You're going home. I'll call you later."

"I did not say please, China, nor did I give you an option. Now, let's go."

The elevator in her mother's building closed around China like a trap—she couldn't get rid of Reeve and she couldn't neglect Clare. In the last few weeks she'd lost control of her life and every ounce of her precious privacy. Reeve appeared calm, leaning on the paneled wall, both hands resting in his hip pockets. Yet the same tension of the last time they had taken this ride together began to invade the tight space and thicken the air. His curt command to her in her apartment had been delivered with the same determination and brusqueness of their first meeting.

What damn-fool antic was Clare up to this time?

Déjà vu was complete in the way Milly whipped the door open before they could knock. "Thank God you got here in time!" She even gave Reeve the same disgusted grunt.

"In time for what?" China was demanding as she raced into the apartment.

"Hey, Singapore! I've missed ya!" There was only one person in the world who called her that. China whipped around and came face-to-face with her half brother, Joey.

"What are you doing here?" China gasped.

"He's AWOL," Milly snapped.

"I wanted to be home for my birthday," Joey said.

"Oh, no," China groaned. "How did you manage this? You couldn't have walked all that way."

"Hitched," Joey boasted. China touched his shoulders as if to prove to herself that he was here and safe. He still wore his gray and blue military uniform and black, spit-shined shoes. The white path of skin outlining his wavy red hair declared a recent visit to the military barber and gave his ears the comical appearance of flying append-ages pasted to each side of his head. He was grinning from ear to ear. It was like looking into Dan Jeffries's face, except for the wide-set gray eyes he and China had inherited from Clare. "The truckers were real nice."

"I don't believe it," China lamented. "You hitchhiked all this way and no one turned you in to the police?"

"Naw. Nobody wants to get involved anymore." He was immensely proud of himself. "Who is this guy?"

China had nearly forgotten Reeve standing at her shoulder. "This is Reeve Laughlin. He's my—" What could she say? "Friend?" It was liable to stick in her throat after spending more of the last two days in the man's bed than she had in her own clothes. "Lover" was out. Joey was barely a teenager. "Clare's lawyer" would be truthfully evasive.

"Our new stepbrother!" Joey exclaimed.

"Why didn't I think of that?" China muttered. Hearing it put in those precise words had the startling sting of a slap in the face. She'd been down this bumpy road before.

Reeve and Joey shook hands. "Martin told me all about you." This revelation not only surprised but hurt China. Martin had never mentioned a son to her. Joey gazed on Reeve with an expression akin to hero-worship. Then his rapt adoration crumbled. "Martin is gone though. Clare just told me."

"Joey," China admonished. "Don't call her Clare. She's your mother, not your pal."

Seeing swift rebellion enter Joey's eyes, Reeve ordered, "Do as your sister says."

"Yes, sir," Joey responded in good military fashion.

Then China tenderly pressed her fingers to Joey's

cheek. "Yes, honey, Martin is gone. I'm sorry; I know you like him. But Reeve thinks he might be back soon." Now, why had she said that? she wondered.

Because the plea in Joey's eyes begged her to. He needed a man in his life, a father figure. And for whatever reason, Joey and Martin had gotten along tremendously; flying kites in Central Park, going fishing in the summer. All the things Martin hadn't done with Reeve, he had made up for with Joey. Yet it was cruel to give the boy hope; even if Martin came back, it didn't mean Clare would keep him.

"China! Darling!" Clare called as she descended the grand staircase. "And Reeve! What a coincidence that you've both dropped in on the same evening. Reeve, you remember my daughter, China, don't you?"

"We came together," Reeve said, while China could only gape at her mother.

"Together," Clare trilled. "What a nice word. So much more intimate than *alone* or *apart*. And look at this, all my children gathered together and it isn't even Thanksgiving yet!" She came tripping down the stairs with Fred falling off each step behind her. Her gown was old, once white, and shredded to bits. She looked like she had been mugged, beaten up, and rolled in the gutter for good measure.

"What's happened to you?" China shrieked.

"Oh, she did that on purpose," Milly said. "And if you don't stop her, the cops will lock her up for attempting murder. She's gonna kill somebody, wait and see if she don't."

"Mother," China began. "*What* are you wearing and— dare I ask—why?"

Three excited voices erupted, and China held her hand up for silence. "I asked *you*, Mother."

"It's Halloween, dear."

China had forgotten. "So it is. And . . . ?"

"I'm going trick-or-treating," Clare announced.

"She is not," Milly snorted. "She's the spirit. The one that's been haunting this building the past five years." Milly crossed her arms over her breasts and thrust her chin out. There was no question about it; Milly was telling the truth. "You know the one!"

Yes, China knew the one. After reports of a recurring ghostlike appearance in the halls of this building, Clare had spearheaded a committee to have it exorcised. The very fact that Clare had financed the ridiculous committee should have told China who this supposed spirit was.

Before China could say anything, Milly went on with her tale. "They's always talk of 'the spirit' the day after she puts that rag on. But now she's got Joey here whispering and giggling and up to something. I don't trust 'em, Miss China."

China turned to Joey, fighting the mental exhaustion slipping around her brain. "Well, what is Milly talking about?"

"This." He held up a bulky portable lamp that was connected to a power pack. "It's a black light."

"And . . ." China prompted.

"I'll show you." Joey walked the few steps to the light switch and plunged the windowless foyer into total darkness. Then he flicked a switch, and China screamed at the sight that confronted her. Clare had been horrendously transformed into a nightmare creature oozing blood, or mud, or some dark, disgusting substance. She looked as if she had actually crawled out of a grave—three years after the burial.

Fred howled like a werewolf at a full moon, and Reeve was heard to mutter an expletive that China would have seconded if she could have found her voice. Then there was a sound. A soft, muted thump that turned her blood to ice water.

"Quick, Joey," China yelled. "The lights, turn on the lights."

Reeve was running past her as the brilliance of the stairwell chandelier burst to life, having identified the chilling sound. There lay Milly, out cold. Her head had struck the first carpeted step of the stairs, saving her from contact with the marble floor and a probable concussion.

While Reeve brought the poor old woman around, China flared up at her mother. "Look what you've done! She's got to be seventy-five or eighty years old. You could have killed her!"

Clare was wide-eyed and looked harmlessly garbed in rags now that Joey had turned the black light off. "It's just special-effects makeup, dear."

Reeve's deep, soothing voice calmed Milly as she rallied, and China bent to the old lady's side to see that she was, indeed, recovering. Milly looked up from the cradle of Reeve's arm and glared at Clare.

"That's it, Mrs. Laughlin. I can't take no more of you. I quit."

Clare waved her arms about, flapping the tattered sleeves. "Fat chance of that, Milly. I tried to get rid of you years ago and you wouldn't go. I'm sure you'll see all of this in a new light in the morning."

"Preferably not a black one," Reeve muttered. Then to China he said, "Where is her bedroom? I'll feel a lot better if we can lay her down on something soft."

"I'll show you. Can you carry her?" China stood and pointed a finger at the other two people in the foyer. "Don't either of you move a muscle until I get back. Mother, you're not going anywhere to scare people out of their wits. And, Joey, you still have to explain what you're doing home without proper leave."

China preceded Reeve, leading him to Milly's bedroom off the kitchen. He was so thorough and calm when he checked Milly over that China believed his assurances that, other than a good shaking up, Milly was fine. When they returned to the foyer, only droopy-eyed Fred could be found. China dashed through the apartment, knowing as she went that Clare and Joey were gone.

"Settle down, China," Reeve finally demanded when he thought she would pace a trench into the floor. "You can't do a damn thing about it until they return."

"She could kill someone pulling that kind of stunt on an unsuspecting soul."

"I doubt it. After all, it's Halloween. People expect to see . . . frightening sights."

"You mean, children dressed up like cowboys and hoboes at the door?" Her words dripped sarcasm. "No one is going to be prepared for that sight, Reeve. No one! It was the most gruesome thing I've ever seen."

It was silent a moment, but only a moment. China recognized the slow-building rumble of his laughter, and her answering scream was a choked sound, strangled in her throat by her own frustration. Reeve quickly turned away from her eye-snapping temper and poured them both a brandy from the living room bar.

"This is not funny, Reeve," China ground out. "And I question the judgment of anyone who thinks it is."

"It is too funny." Reeve brought her the brandy. "And I question the judgment of anyone who doesn't see the humor in it. If I hadn't spent the weekend with a woman so enthralling that I forgot the days of the week, I might be out ringing a few doorbells myself. I make up into a very convincing Frankenstein's monster."

China couldn't work up the enthusiasm to play quick-witted games. She took the snifter from him and carried it to the window where she set it on the ledge. Crushing the Chinese silk drapes in her fists, she stared through the glass, wondering how long before the delinquent pair would return.

"Why don't you call Joey's school?" Reeve suggested. "Let them know he arrived here safely."

The fact that the staff was only just now discovering that Joey was missing when China's call came through had them sufficiently embarrassed to grant concessions. Without being specific, China hinted at a serious family problem having upset Joey so much that he had suddenly needed the stabilizing comfort of hearth and home. Heavens, if they only knew the truth! With China's promise to escort him personally back on Wednesday morning, they grudgingly agreed to let Joey remain through his Tuesday birthday, adding the severe warning that "Mr. Jeffries will walk five hours on the parade field."

Scuffling feet announced the return of mother and son. China raced to the archway leading into the living room and Joey and Clare stumbled into each other when they confronted China's glare. "You will both come in here, please."

They had the good grace to hang their heads penitently. Clare glided over to the bar and poured herself a cognac while Joey took the seat adjacent to Reeve, his feet planted flat on the floor, his elbows resting on his knees, and his hands hanging between his open legs.

"First off," China began, "did you hurt anyone?"

"Of course not," Clare reported. Meeting China's skeptical side-glance, she said, "Ask your brother if you don't believe me."

"Is he supposed to be your character witness?"

"It was fun," Joey said. "Most people were scared at first, but then they laughed."

"That's true, dear," Clare insisted. "It's nice to know others appreciated the trouble we went to."

China choked the back of a chair with fingers that trembled with rage. "Joey, I've spoken with the academy and they've agreed to give you leave until Wednesday.

Then I will personally take you back there. You'll be responsible for whatever schoolwork you missed, and you've been given five hours to walk."

"But, China—"

"No buts," she cut him off. "You and Clare can celebrate your joint birthdays Tuesday night, and then you're going back to school."

Joey looked up and his eyes caught the warning in Reeve's blue gaze. "Yes, ma'am," he responded.

"It's late. Go on to bed now." China dismissed him.

Joey stood and reached out to shake Reeve's hand. "It's been great meeting you. Will you come to dinner with us on Tuesday? Clare . . . uh, I mean, Mother and I have the same birthday. I'm going to be fourteen."

"I'd like that very much, Joey. It isn't every day a man discovers he has a brother." Reeve smiled.

"Oh, China and I get a new one every time Mother marries."

"So I've been told," Reeve said dryly.

Once Joey's footsteps had faded away, China turned to her mother. She was determined to be kind. All the same, Clare had to be stopped from behavior like tonight's. And this haunting of the building couldn't go on. "What do you have to say for yourself, Mother?"

"Well, I'd like to know how long you and Reeve have been keeping company." As usual, Clare's train of thought ran on a one-way track.

Reeve amiably answered the question before China could silently signal him not to. "China and I have been *keeping* each other since the day you brought us together, Clare."

Clare beamed. "How wonderful."

China winced at Reeve's stress on *keeping* and Clare's hopeful expression. "I object to this," China began, attempting to turn the conversation back to its starting point.

"On what grounds?" Reeve demanded.

Startled, China shot her glance at him. "It's immaterial."

"Trying to use your *Late Show* courtroom education against a pro like me, honey?" His dark brow shot up with an unspoken dare.

What was he doing? China asked herself. "Immaterial is a perfectly legitimate maneuver, isn't it? And it applies here, doesn't it?"

An abrupt nod of his head conceded the point, and China continued.

"Well, Mother, you certainly are reverting to childhood. I don't know what to do about you anymore. Don't you feel the least bit responsible for Joey? For the kind of example you're setting for him?"

"Object," Reeve bounded out of his seat. "Badgering the witness." The serious words had a very definite thread of amusement running through them.

China still had her mouth open when he burst forth and now she furiously spun on him. "What are you defending her for?"

"I'm her attorney."

Clare took advantage of China's momentary stupor to jump in. "And you are acting just like a nasty prosecutor, China. I'm fortunate to have Reeve here."

"You know, Reeve, your crazy behavior is making my mother look sensible." China shook her head in disgust and turned back to Clare. "You will corrupt that boy if you continue so recklessly to—"

"Object," Reeve snapped again, and China wanted to throw something at him. "You'll have to rephrase that as a question."

"Overruled," Clare said. "Oh, I do so enjoy a good parlor game. But, Reeve, I'd like to speak to that if I may."

"I'll withdraw my objection then."

Between the two of them, China was ready to wave the white flag and surrender.

The gray shade of Clare's eyes that usually resembled a thick fog cleared to sharp slate. It was a phenomenon that rarely occurred but when it did, China suspected that an intelligent woman had been locked away inside Clare's brain. "I'm setting the same example for Joey that I set for you when you were growing up. And look how you turned out. You're a sensible girl—a little too uptight for my taste—but you've got your head on straight, as they say these days. You work a steady job, pay your bills on time. Why, you even fold your socks. So I didn't do such a bad job with you, did I? And no use trying to say it was your father who made you so stable. According to the experts, a child's character is well formed by the time it's five years old, and your father was hardly around until you were ten. He had his office and his clients and his stocks and bonds. *I* raised you and I raised you well.

"As for Joey, he's well past the age of having his character built or destroyed. He pulls very good marks in school and is turning out to be as responsible as you are . . . he just has a little more fun in life than you do. So you can stop worrying about your brother."

It was the longest speech China had ever heard from her mother. She was well aware that she had been sweetly told off. In fact, Clare made her sound downright boring! "And besides," Clare put in one more for good measure, "if you would give me a grandchild to indulge, I wouldn't be forced to spoil Joey. And you could quit practicing your maternal instincts on me. It's very tiring for me, dear."

"Enough said," Reeve remarked. "You've questioned your mother enough for one night, China. Come, I'll take you home."

China was suddenly exhausted and retreated simply

because she was not mentally armed to do efficient battle with Clare *and* Reeve.

Clare saw them to the door. Just as they were about to step out, she riveted Reeve's attention as her soft, thready voice questioned, "Martin?"

Reeve folded a large hand over Clare's knitted fingers. "My private detective will catch up with him in a day or two. I'll let you know."

"I see." Clare nodded, wistfulness clouding her eyes. "Tell Dick Tracy to shoot first, ask questions later."

Reeve smiled tenderly at Clare. "I'll deliver the message."

China, fed up with both of them, marched to the elevator and held the door for Reeve.

"There is one more thing," Clare said, stalling Reeve's departure. Her eyes slid to China standing in the elevator, and she lowered her voice so that only Reeve could hear her. "I've been thinking, wondering . . . well, there was all that talk of financial arrangements the first time you two were here. I couldn't stand it if any daughter of mine . . . what I mean is . . . she isn't charging you, is she?"

"She is not!" Reeve snapped. Then a laugh of pure enjoyment shook his broad chest. "Although she is costing me a great deal."

"I know what you mean. I do worry so about her, Reeve. But I'll rest easier knowing she has someone like you to watch out for her." Then Clare closed the door.

Eleven

The Off-Off-Broadway theater on the south side of Manhattan was half empty. China sat on a serviceable folding chair listening to water pipes clank. She huddled deep in her coat as the heat seeped out of the boarded-up windows faster than it could seep into the gutted room.

The play, the plot of which continued to escape her, was nearing the end of the first act, and the particular actress she had come to see had a walk-on just before the intermission. She had it from a reliable source that this fresh new face, a recent arrival from Milwaukee, was not only very talented but also unagented. In the meantime China was subjected to watching the male lead feign sleep on a center-stage bed as the lights slowly, interminably, lowered to full blackout, then just as slowly reversed, simulating the passage of night.

A follow-spot hopped around the stage, creating a light-display on the floorboards before finding its mark.

The male lead bolted upright to yawn and stretch in the glare of theatrically affected sunrise. China sat up straighter. This was the cue for the girl she had come to see.

The pretty starlet, a leggy young redhead, strolled across the stage to deliver to the lead actor his breakfast in bed. She had potential, China thought: good carriage and an easy, sensual stride. Noticeably thin, she would find that to her advantage in television and film because the camera added ten pounds or so to an actor's figure. The redhead's purring speech was pure femininity; she had clear enunciation and her voice was a bit husky. Perfect for "intimate" commercials—lingerie, perfume, personal hygiene. Thirty million people might be her audience, but her voice had that "just-between-you-and-me" quality.

China flipped her typed program to the back. She penned a brief message for the actress to contact her at her office, folded her business card inside, and scooted forward on her chair to leave.

Another character entered the bedroom scene from stage right and there was something about the lead actor's widening eyes and dropped chin that made China wonder what was happening that shouldn't be happening.

A man in a navy sweatshirt and faded jeans, affecting the stiff, steel-spine gait of a butler, walked up to the bed.

"Reeve!" she gasped in surprise. Four heads turned to glare at her when she cried out.

He didn't look her way, but China saw him bite his lower lip to keep from smiling.

"Uh . . . uh—" The poor bed-ridden actor hadn't the slightest idea what was going on.

"James, sir," Reeve prompted.

"Of course, James," the lead cried.

Reeve bowed low and extended a postcard-size slip of paper to the man. "An invitation."

Trembling fingers took the extended paper and confused eyes checked both sides of what had to be an empty card.

China giggled. A harried voice offstage could be heard: "What the hell is going on out there?" China laughed louder.

"Shhh . . ." A man two rows up turned to glare at her, and she grew contritely silent. China fixed her eyes on Reeve's angular features, lovingly tracing his profile with her gaze as he delivered another line.

"Your mother's lawyer begs you to share a cup of coffee and congenial conversation with him."

"Coffee?" The harried actor didn't know what to do next. "Well, sure." His gaze searched the dark wings. "Show him in."

"He'd like you to join him across the street at the diner." Hard as it was to believe, Reeve's impromptu performance actually improved the play.

Sweat gathered on the actor's brow and upper lip. "Yes!" he exclaimed, hoping to be rid of Reeve.

"Yes!" China echoed, knowing the invitation was meant for her.

"Aw, lady, shut up," her front-row critic muttered. "Some people wanna see the play."

China could only stare at Reeve up there on stage. She was in love with him, she told herself. Heaven help her, but it was true. Last night, leaning on the hold button of the elevator and watching Reeve and Clare with their heads bent together, she had known it. Gratitude, she told herself—not love! The fingers of reason tried to flick the sentiment away. Persistently, like a small seed lost in fertile earth, it grew, the roots stretching down to wrap tenaciously around her heart.

Overwhelmed by him. Seduced by him. Sexually gratified by him. She told herself all these things and more in the lonely space of her anemic apartment. Long, restless hours trying to settle reckless, churning thoughts. She admitted she loved him; she denied it. Back and forth until dawn. With her fists jammed to her eye sockets, she replayed their weekend together and every smoky, baritone word he had said to her as she lay blanketed with the passion-drenched scent of him. She loved him.

The Act One curtain dropped, literally, with a thud. China rushed from her seat, giving the usher at the door her note and business card for the young actress before she ran out on the street to look for Reeve. China drank in the crisp night air and felt warmer. Damp, poorly heated buildings bit to the bone with sharper teeth than the real elements, even if it was several degrees colder outside. It was a clear star-splattered night except for a rainbow haze circling the platinum moon, warning of rain on the morrow.

Reeve stepped out from the stage-door alley and China walked toward him, laughing. "You're crazy, you know that? I never know what you'll do next!"

"It isn't fun if you know ahead of time." His eyes traced her fine features with all the possessive emotions she felt when she looked at him. "You're staring again," he whispered.

She grinned, nodding. Slipping under his sinewy arm, she melted against him. "You sure you don't want to do print work? You could make me rich and famous."

"You're already rich and famous." He snorted, turning her around and walking her down the curb into the street. "Why didn't you answer my messages? You know I hate talking to that damn machine."

"I haven't been home. I went from the office to a working dinner with an ad client, then straight here. How did you find me?"

He dropped his mouth to her ear, the brush of his lips

on the curled shell an intoxicating touch, drugging her senses and leaving her slightly light-headed. "When you didn't answer the messages I left on your infernal machine, I called your office and Marce said you'd be here."

"What time was that?"

"About seven-thirty."

China grimaced. "Marce works too hard. She should have gone home long before that."

An overhead streetlight flashed off his jaw and chin, and the casual fall of black hair over his high brow lent him an appealing, rakish air. He wore a sheepskin jacket over his habitual nonworking-hours ensemble of jeans, sweatshirt, and tennis shoes.

"Feel like that cup of coffee?" he asked.

"Do I look like that cup of coffee?" she quipped. "Actually I feel like a frozen Popsicle."

The sweep of his gaze encompassed the swirling pattern of her red and white dress, her white angora jacket, and her jaunty red cap. "You look like a strawberry parfait." His arms crept around her waist, his hands slipping under her jacket to mold her to him. "And you feel like a toasted marshmallow, warm to the touch and full of melting sweetness."

It wasn't until after they were seated and Reeve had instructed the waitress to bring two coffees that China thought to question the situation. Why had they come here? Reeve's loft was only two blocks away, and China knew from making Sunday morning's breakfast that he was well supplied with coffee. Then there was the fact that he had left messages on her machine when he had previously refused to leave so much as his name on it.

"China, you think transparently. It's no wonder I bested you at chess."

"Something is wrong," she said in a leaden voice.

"Because I brought you here instead of my loft."

"Something urgent?"

"Nothing to be alarmed about. However, time is limited, and a cup of coffee is not all we might share if I took you home. I have to go out of town tonight. I should have left an hour ago. I'll be back for the birthday celebration tomorrow, though I may be cutting it close. I'll meet you at Clare's apartment."

"You mean, you're leaving right now? This late at night?"

"Driving," he confirmed. "I hope to reach my destination before midnight."

"Who has meetings at mid—" Suddenly China knew whom he was meeting. He had found his father.

"Reeve," China murmured, staring down into her coffee mug. "Do something for me? Keep Martin away until Wednesday. Don't let him intrude on tomorrow night. No confrontations until I get Joey back to school."

"Queenie, you do work your trusty soldier hard." His brooding gaze studied her, flinching at the naked plea in her waiting expression. And as he looked across the spray-and-wipe Formica, something in him snapped. "For goodness' sakes, China, who am I defending you from? First there was Clare, threatening to kill Martin without a second thought, presuming there was ever a first one! Then I had the *dis*pleasure of meeting Doctor Paul, your in-need-of-a-psychiatrist psychiatrist. So along with humoring your mother out of committing murder, I find myself trying to deck your ex-husband. Mind you, this from a man who signed away ten years of his future earnings as collateral to learn how to settle disputes peaceably in a court of law. And now Clare's husband too? Does it extend to past as well as present stepfathers? It's turning into one man against an army."

"Are you blaming me?" China exploded. "Who ever asked you to be my defender? I certainly didn't. I did just fine for thirty years without you. In fact, I warned you not to dance to Clare's music. If it wasn't for your meddling, Martin wouldn't be coming back here. So you can just call in your investigator, Mr. Knight in Shining Armor, and head back to your SoHo fortress. I don't need you."

She hadn't realized she was crying until he reached across the table to cup her chin in his palm and thumbed the wet streaks on her cheeks. "Don't, babe. I'm sorry. Please don't cry."

This, of course, made more tears slip over her lashes. "You're so strong and confident, China. So independent. Then the phone rings or a name is mentioned or a columnist hits with a low blow, and you start clenching your fists as if your sanity will slip away from you if you let go. I wish you could separate yourself from all those fears."

For all her spouting that she didn't need him, she wanted very much to dump the whole mess in his competent lap—lock, stock, and extended family. "Reeve, don't bring Martin back."

"But I thought you wanted him found before Clare calls out the hit men after him?"

She turned her head to look out the window and saw her pain-etched reflection in the glass. "I don't know. I don't know anymore what I want. But Martin doesn't want to come back. Why force it?"

"Martin left a better trail than Hansel and Gretel. I'll keep him under wraps though. The confrontation of the generals will be postponed until Joey has been evacuated." He raised his hand up to support his vow. "I promise."

And Reeve always kept his promises, China told herself.

Pressed for time, he hailed a cab, kissed her good-bye,

and gave the cabby China's address. She watched him out the rear window until the taxi turned the corner.

Marce ran across the column in the Tuesday-morning edition, folded the paper back to the article, and placed it on China's desk.

Slumping down to her chair, China glared at the offending newsprint, praying she had her thick skin on. She stared at the picture of Reeve, a dated yearbook photo, and the one of her next to it. Her picture, if she remembered correctly, had been run before, and Paul had been standing next to her. They had severed his hand when they had lopped him off and it could still be seen curled at her waist.

Taking a deep breath, she began to read:

The mother-daughter duo are up to their old tricks, Darlings. Remember when our incorrigible Clarissa was Mrs. Arthur Payne (if you can, Sweets) and she dressed her little China in outfits made to match her own designer duds? Seems it was habit-forming and led to their wearing the same names—both later wedded their way to the title of Mrs. Paul Doran. (Tiffany's could never keep the charge accounts straight.) Clarissa turned in the name Jeffries (#4) for Laughlin (#5) last summer and rumor has it China may do the same soon. (Relax, Tiffany's. The first names are different this time.) China has been seen up, down, and all around town with her stepfather's son, Reeve. The younger Mr. Laughlin is a partner at the prestigious law firm Hoffer, Kole—if Clarissa plays her cards right she may get her divorces free in the future. And the noticeable absence of the senior Laughlin from their

West Side apartment hints to the possibility of that event happening soon.

China, darling, pay no attention to tasteless jokes. After seeing your Reeve, this columnist would take him if he were her real honest-to-goodness brother. He's to die for, dear. . . .

China swallowed. She hoped she wouldn't vomit. The whole thing made her sound spoiled and shallow, not to mention immoral. And Reeve. What would Reeve think? How would he feel?

China glanced up to see Marce framed in the doorway. China dumped the paper in the garbage where it belonged. "Has Mr. Laughlin left a message on the service?" China asked.

"No. Don't let it get to you, China. Your friends don't believe that crap if they even bother to read it, and your enemies will think it whether they read it or not."

Intellectually China knew what Marce said was true. Unfortunately her heart was suffering from a low I.Q. "Bring me work to do. Lots of work."

The day dragged on. China drove Marce crazy asking if Reeve had telephoned. If she left the office for a mere five minutes, she dashed back convinced she had missed his call. By late afternoon Marce greeted her returns with her head already shaking in the negative. China even placed two calls to Hoffer, Kole only to be told by a confounded Debra Wendell that it was no different there.

At home her answering machine was as frustratingly unenlightening. She listened to the playback while leaning on the open refrigerator door, scanning the meager contents for a light snack to tide her over until the birthday celebration. A bottle of Chablis on the top shelf was the only item to interest her. Why not? There were only a few healthy mouthfuls left.

Uncorking the wine, she put her lips to the rim and took a swig, then walked barefoot to the living room, dangling the bottle by its narrow neck. The pillows and plants were an underwhelming attempt at trying to make this ice palace a home, China concluded. The weekend with Reeve had altered her focus . . . her fears. Her world had turned topsy-turvy, the problems becoming reversed in the tumble.

What if Clare *didn't* divorce Martin? Or annul the marriage? Reeve would be her stepbrother. How would she survive the breakup with Reeve if she had to sit down to family Christmas dinner and look across the table at the man who had been her lover?

Maybe Paul was right. Maybe she needed a psychiatrist. What if she didn't love Reeve but was self-destructively bent on repeating her own history? Draining the bottle as she walked, she relegated the dry vessel to the kitchen wastebasket.

It was time to get dressed.

Exquisite was the only word for the black beaded cocktail dress. Love at first sight was how the outrageously expensive frock found its way to China's closet. Epaulettes of ink-slick bugle beads capped her shoulders and dripped down the diaphanous sleeves of the dusky chiffon overdress. A two-inch border of the same shimmering beads weighted down the hem of the curve-clinging fabric. Her nylons were luxuriously sheer, and the discerning eye was lured to the slim turn of her right ankle by a small butterfly appliqué.

Rose-red lipstick and nail polish were the only splashes of color from her fashionably strappy black shoes to sleekly knotted raven hair. Tucking two gift-wrapped presents under her arm, China slid a fur-trimmed jacket off its hanger and left the apartment.

The cab deposited her at the Central Park entrance to her mother's building as the first rolling swell of thunder tumbled across the sky. The thought of Reeve, upstairs, waiting for her, drew her gaze up the brick and mortar facade to the rectangles of golden windows on the sixth floor.

Milly greeted China and took her jacket. Reeve, she was informed, had just phoned to say he would meet them at the restaurant.

"Why? Did he say why?" China snapped it so fast that Milly jumped.

"Course, he did. 'Cause he can't meet you here."

Milly is old, China reasoned, gripping the shreds of her ragged nerves and forcing a smile. "I realize that much. But did you ask him *why* he had to change his plans?"

"Not my business. Besides, he's a Laughlin, ain't he? Who knows why they do the things they do? Go along to the library now before your mum gets that boy of hers sloshed."

Actually Joey was toasting his fourteenth year with a harmless glass of ginger ale. He looked very grown-up in brass-buttoned military dress, China thought. She imprinted a lipstick kiss on his forehead and gave him his birthday present.

With Clare she neatly touched cheeks. "You look stunning tonight, Mother." Clare's soft wool dress repeated the golden chestnut of her hair. A weave of silver threads swirled from waist to shoulder, an echo of the perfectly coiffed silver streak in her hair. It was classically Clare.

"And you, dear . . . considering." Clare was subdued with sympathy. She was probably the only person in the world from whom China could take that particular look right now. The most caustic exposé about her only coaxed bubbles of laughter from Clare—but never when her children were the victims.

"Fantastic!" Joey exclaimed, opening his gift and sliding the stereo headphones over his ears.

Clare blinked, astounded. "That's one hell of a set of earmuffs, China!"

The absurdity of the mistake made China laugh, and she explained about the radio headset. Clare opened her own gift next, and as much as she admired the slim, gold stickpin, it was the headphones she fell in love with.

"Reeve called to say he will meet us at the restaurant," China informed her mother, thinking it wise not to mention Martin at all.

"Milly," Clare called into the foyer. "Call the garage and have them send the car around."

The storm clouds had opened to release fat, gentle raindrops. The doorman escorted them singly under his umbrella to the customized limousine. By the time they reached the restaurant, a stiff wind was driving a rain sheet sideways, and pitchfork lightning stabbed the sky.

Profuse greetings were bestowed on the familial trio before the maître d' led them to the inner sanctum and the best table in the house. Generations of social and financial distinction were required in order to reserve a table at this most exclusive café. It made for a predestined crowd of regulars. Unless a woman married several rungs up the social ladder, she was forever known here by her maiden name. China cynically appreciated the custom, given the game of musical husbands played by this set—a consistent title saved many a maître d' from an excruciatingly embarrassing situation.

Arriving at their table, China pivoted and saw Reeve walk in. She was pulled a half step in his direction, drawn to his potent maleness by an invisible braid of emotions: ropes of raw need, strings of sweet yearning, and threads of a tenuous, blossoming love.

Heads turned to look at the new man, and many a feminine brow arched in ambitious interest. Even China found herself unexpectedly short of breath. The black-tie elegance of his formal attire magnified the hard-boned, lean-muscled body it was meant to conceal. His brilliant gaze locked with her gentle eyes. The manner in which he stalked her turned a bevy of venturesome gleams to undeniable envy.

Claiming China's hand in an electrifying clasp, he directed his attention to the guests of honor. Clare made a complicated affair out of choreographing the seating, making more production of it than was necessary for four people.

Having finally been assigned, China turned, the small movement placing her cheek in physical contact with the angular slope of Reeve's jaw. His warm hands gripped her waist, the fingers digging slightly to tumble her gently into his arms.

"Oh, don't," she begged.

"We haven't said a proper hello." His voice was as smooth as cream, the mouth that swooped down on hers as on-target as a diving hawk on a field mouse. China felt the same nowhere-to-run trap of the victim too. The back and forth sweep of his lips coaxed her to yield the entrance he sought even as she inwardly shrank from the many eyes on them.

Her teeth tested the give of his tongue, resulting in Reeve's prudent withdrawal. Pure devilry met her infuri-ated glare. She hated spectacular displays that made her the star attraction of the evening!

"No, I won't apologize for kissing you," he drawled. "You asked for it in that drop-dead dress."

"Oh? You look pretty steady on your feet."

"Barely, sweetheart, and hanging on for dear life."

China turned her upper body while her hips were still molded to his. Clare and Joey were grinning, the head-waiter was open-mouthed, and throughout the silk-papered room lips were furiously flapping behind raised hands.

The flash of a pen scraping paper at a nearby table caused China to drop inelegantly in her seat. Tonight, of all nights, a reporter had to be dining here! Reeve sat to China's right and Joey to her left at the round table, placing Clare across from her. When she thought her composure had been restored, she glanced over the leather-bound menu. The haggard lines reaching out from Reeve's eyes startled her. She wanted to reach out and smooth them away. Had last night not gone well? Or was it the scurrilous article? Surely someone would have told him about it. China knew only too well how fast bad news was delivered by "good" friends. Oh, if only they could have a few minutes alone!

A small orchestra tucked in an obscure corner discreetly tuned their instruments as the foursome gave their dinner orders to the waiter. He departed as the first beckoning strains of a waltz floated through the room. The dance floor was filling—the perfect solution.

"Reeve, dance with me?"

He glanced up from sipping his Scotch. "Now?"

"Now," she repeated.

"Now?" Clare sputtered. "China, the salad will come anytime."

"Now," China insisted. "How long does one tune last? Two, maybe three minutes."

Reeve plucked his napkin from his lap and laid it on the table. "If you'll excuse us, Clare." He followed China, his voice low and intimate. "Experience has taught me that a woman who needs only two or three minutes to be satisfied is too impatient to be kept waiting."

China threaded her way through the tables to the small dance floor, provoked to a slow seethe. Didn't he take anything seriously? She turned and stepped into his arms.

He danced as he did everything else—with skillful precision. He pulled her close, crushing the starched ruffles of his dress shirt, and she realized that he was going to kiss her again. Craning her head back, she shook it. "I wish you hadn't kissed me earlier. There is a reporter at that table near the door. I don't relish having half the city know where my lips were the night before."

"Is this what you were champing at the bit to do? Bawl me out?"

"I don't like reading about myself, Reeve." Her eyes were flecked with silver, mirrors of the questions splintering through her head.

"Yes, babe, I got all the gory details. Martin read the column to me as we were driving into the city this afternoon. Bob Hoffer read it to me again earlier this evening. Rough, wasn't it? I am a convert to your contempt for the press, not uncommon with victims."

A supreme understatement, Reeve thought. A blind man seeing daylight would have been as stunned. Reeve hadn't been prepared for the depth of anger exposed by the invasion into his private affairs. Even Martin, who rarely felt encumbered by life's shoulds or should nots rankled at the vulgar nature of the article.

"So Martin is back in the city." There was no mistaking the hard veneer coating her words.

"Try to be charitable to him, China. He's not the dashing, debonair fortune-hunter I last saw two years ago. He's older, sadder, and very lonely. For Clare mostly, but for me also. I think you and I are guilty of extremes and need to learn to strike a happy medium. You've hovered too much and I need to be more attentive."

Was this the same man who had washed his hands of his father? "Will Martin stay out of sight until tomorrow?"

"Didn't I promise you?"

He slid his hand down her back, sensuously exploring

over the gauzy chiffon. He loved the feel of her in his arms, the sway of her flared hips moving to the music. Just as he began to melt around her, she bristled and stiffly fought his embrace.

A relentless smile hovered in his black-lashed eyes. "I don't care if there is a reporter at the door; a man can kiss his fiancée. Nothing scandalous about that, is there?"

China felt her heart jump into her throat and was only able to gulp it back down when she realized he was mocking that ridiculous rumor in the newspaper that she might soon change her name to Laughlin.

"Harrumph," China grunted. "If Clare married every rumor printed in that same column, she'd have had a dozen husbands by now."

"And here Bob Hoffer and I have already toasted my engagement. He won't like this bit of news."

"Bob? What's he got to do with it? Tell him not to believe what he reads." China saw the waiter serving their dinner and began to move out of Reeve's arms to return to the table.

"I don't think that will work." Reeve touched his lips to her ear to whisper "Not after they found a pair of stray underwear in the law library."

"Oh, my God!" China gasped. Embarrassment poured color into her cheeks and she hid her face in his shoulder. "Wait a minute," China drawled thoughtfully. Then her narrowed gaze slid to Reeve. "I wasn't wearing underwear."

"Right. It wasn't yours."

"Yours!" She started laughing as Reeve swooped her back into his arms. "Come on, Reeve. You don't expect me to believe he took one look at them and knew who they belonged to. Not unless you had your name in them."

"I had my name in the guard's register, and—"

"And you introduced me as your sister." She groaned. Talk about incest! "Well, I won't get married just because some reporter announced it in the paper." *She wouldn't.* Even if she *had* learned to love his unpredictable behavior and *he* had learned how demeaning it was to be gossiped about.

"Why not, China?" He pierced her with his blue gaze.

"Why not? Three days ago you reminded me how temporary relationships are. I'm not interested in a limited-run marriage." A marriage that his boss wanted more than he did to make him respectable enough to remain a Hoffer, Kole partner, she fumed.

A piercing scream from across the room put an abrupt end to any talk of marriage. So riveting was the scream that a deathlike silence fell over the room, all eyes clinging to the person from whom it had issued.

"You bastard. . . . You lousy son of a—" Clare was standing and screeching like a steam whistle. "Why you . . . you . . . you've got a hell of a nerve. . . ." A plate whirled across the room and crashed to the dance floor, shattering into tiny fragments. A spray of yellow béarnaise sauce speckled the ribbon-tied oak.

Three feet from where the dish had landed China saw Martin, as dashing and debonair as ever. "Oh, no!" The eyes she turned to Reeve were twin pools of accusation as Clare began another vituperative harangue. "You promised . . . you promised," China kept repeating.

"Don't jump to conclusions, China. You're liable to land on the wrong assumption. Stay calm."

All around China were scurrying waiters and stunned patrons. The maître d' was horror-stricken. And she was supposed to stay calm?

Martin lithely danced his way free of the continuing barrage of plates. Joey's Dover sole joined China's lobster thermidor. The polished dance floor was buried under inches of thick sauce, shards of crockery, and clumps of undefinable food.

"Now, sweet," Martin crooned. He stooped quickly, throwing an arm up as a platter sailed over his head to land with a resounding crash behind him. "Clare, sweetheart. . . . I know you're a mite upset. . . ." He sidestepped a fistful of spoons Clare grabbed off the tray of a paralyzed waiter. ". . . and you've every right to be. But, I'm back, dear. . . ."

China buried her face in her hands. "Damn you, Reeve. You promised me."

Seeing that Martin was closing in on Clare and presuming the worst of it was over, Reeve turned to China. "I didn't have anything to do with his coming here."

"Oh, he just happened to be passing by and happened to be hungry and happened to drop in here for dinner."

"I didn't tell him where I was going tonight. He must have talked to Milly."

The maître d' was busy writing on a tablet, and China could only assume he was tallying the destruction. "Help me get them out of here," China snapped, wrenching out of Reeve's arms.

Staring straight ahead, ignoring the vicarious glee in the faces she passed, China headed for the table. "Joey, gather Mother's things. Mother, put that butter knife down. For heaven's sake, it won't even penetrate the man's suit coat."

Martin gently disarmed Clare of the blunt-edged knife just as a parade of oblivious waiters exited the kitchen with a birthday cake, singing "Happy Birthday." In the same instant that China realized what Clare would do next, so did Martin. He ducked and the cake landed in the lap of a woman at the next table.

China turned to the maître d' at her elbow. "Add the dress to our bill." Then she started to cry. Tears welled up in her eyes and ran down her face. She had never felt so mortified, so publicly humiliated, so helpless. The next thing she knew they were out on the street, the Porsche and limousine at the curb. Joey took one look at Reeve's Porsche and climbed into the front seat. China found herself in the limousine, sitting across from Clare and Martin.

They cuddled and cooed like lovebirds. All forgiven and forgotten. China could only stare at them.

Back at Clare's apartment Joey gave Milly a blow-by-blow of the night's events, sounding like the announcer at a Sugar Ray Leonard fight. Reeve had taken Clare and Martin to the seclusion of the library to tidy up the final details of the reconciliation.

China slipped out the door and into the elevator. The doorman rushed outside to whistle up a taxi while she restlessly paced the marble lobby. A rainy night in New York made cabs a scarce commodity. When the elevator opened once again to let Reeve out, China dashed outside into the rain. The determined downpour had eased to a softly drenching shower.

Reeve called out and her pace quickened. She squished into two puddles for every three steps she took. She ran across the street and into Central Park. "China, where do you think you're going? You'll catch your death of cold if you don't get yourself mugged first."

"That would be one way to avoid what they'll print in tomorrow's paper! Stay away from me, Reeve. I'm going home."

"We have to talk."

"Not tonight. No talking tonight."

Sensing that, if crowded, she might scurry off into the dangerous interior of the park, he followed at a distance. "I asked you to marry me, China."

"And I refused." God, why did it hurt so much to say that? "I was going to have a one-and-only husband, not a list that had to be numerically ordered. I'm a loser at marriage, Reeve. We both are."

"We're not losers together. I'm good for you, China."

"So I've noticed as I walk in a Central Park war zone, in the middle of the night, in a freezing rain, ruining an original designer dress. Pay close attention to my irrational behavior as I have a nervous breakdown."

"You love me, China, and I love you." His words reached and calmed her. They also made her incredibly sad.

"That isn't enough." She turned to face him. "I felt that for Paul, too. You loved Ann. But it didn't last. It never does." She tipped her face up to the cool rain and closed her eyes to the drops splashing down. He'd never see her tears for the streaks of rain.

"We can try it together, China. And if we try hard enough—"

"*Try* marriage? For size, like a dress? For fit, like a shoe? I could keep my apartment, just in case. We could write up a prenuptial agreement; that way the divorce will be all set, we just activate the terms when the time is right. A marriage with a built-in failure factor! No. No, thanks."

"Why won't you marry me, China? Dammit, why?"

"Because ending a love affair is easier than ending a marriage. You don't give as much to a lover, so you don't lose as much at the end."

During the exchange, Reeve had slowly approached her. Now, China backed away, coming to a gate and exiting the park. She scanned the streets for a cab, and Reeve, seeing her desperation, whistled. Magically a yellow on-duty cab pulled up. China glared at it. He always did everything so perfectly! She stood at the door of the cab, hesitating.

"Are you sending me away?" Reeve asked, walking up to her.

When she looked at him, really looked at him—at his ocean-blue eyes that washed over her, at the formidable shoulders that supported her so gently, at the hands that knew every inch of her body—she couldn't bear not to see him again.

"No, Reeve, I'm not sending you away. I just won't marry you. Tonight I want to go home and get some sleep. Tomorrow I'll see you."

"No, China," he said softly, mournfully. "I won't be your lover. I'll be your love, your husband, but not your lover. I told you the day we met that I expect a lot more than meals and midnights for a percentage of me. I want all of you, China."

"And what do I get? You're asking for an awful lot without promising much in return."

He was close enough that he was able to haul her to the wall of his chest in one lightning-fast jerk. The hands gripping her arms were painful, his eyes ice-blue as they bore into hers. His snarling voice was a knife in her heart. "Name your price. Ann came pretty damn expensive for the little she gave back. But you . . . you can write yourself one hell of a ticket. There isn't a man on earth who wants a woman as badly as I want you. Be as extravagant as you please; I'll pay. But I get a hundred percent of you for it."

The flat of her hands pushed at his chest. But his hold resisted her struggles, so she stopped fighting and said in a challenging voice, "Children. I want children."

He let go of her. "Insurance. Go on, call it by its rightful name. You don't want children, you want insurance. You can't take one damn step forward or backward without a promise." He took one last sad look at her. "Is there anyone you trust, China?"

She stared at his retreating back for a long time before folding herself into the cab. He loved her. Despite the cruel words just spoken, she knew he loved her. Too much to stay away long. He'd come back.

They would have their season together and love each other for as long as it lasted. And no one, *no one*, would watch the inevitable parting. Her memory flew back to the reporters at the courthouse when her divorce was finalized.

Never again. If she and Reeve had a month, a year, or ten years to share passion and love, then China would greedily wring every drop of pleasure from it. But when it was over, as it seemed destined to be, there would not be lawyers and courts and divorce decrees and the press. China would at least have the comfort of privacy when the time came to live through the hell of losing Reeve.

Tomorrow . . . tomorrow he would call. They'd apologize and make love. He loved her too much not to come back.

Twelve

Arctic November winds howled outside her office windows. The subzero temperatures had slipped into China's soul, putting her emotions on ice, anesthetizing the heartache. Not even Marce's incandescent smile radiated enough warmth to melt the protective freeze. "As I see it," Marce said, rolling out a long tube of blueprints across China's desk, "you've got two options."

"Sign the contract, or sign the contract," China quipped half-heartedly. The Payne Agency had just beaten out the rest of the entertainment industry by winning the coveted contract to cast a major motion picture epic the likes of which hadn't been made in years. The key phrase being: *featuring a cast of thousands*. And ten percent of every actor, from flat-rate extras to multimillion-dollar stars, belonged to China.

"The suite of offices next to yours will be vacant shortly," Marce went on. "The architect says he can break through here"—Marce pointed out scratches on the plans—"and double your square footage. Or an insurance firm is moving out of a generous setup on the twenty-eighth floor."

"Do I really want more space? More agents?"

"Do you really want to fall flat on your face trying to do this huge production alone? The architect will meet you for lunch tomorrow and take you on a tour of your options." Receiving China's nod of agreement, Marce rolled up the prints and headed for the door, pausing on the threshold.

China pretended interest in the accumulation of snow dusting her windowsill. Peripherally she saw Marce tilt her head, her brow knit with worry. The young girl breathed a sigh of weary concern before closing the door behind her. The blistering column relating the events of the birthday fiasco had had ten days to cool. It was not uncommon for China to withdraw for a week or two after one of these publicly aired humiliations. Sometimes longer.

Her reserved mood was never a plea for sympathy, but rather an honest demand to be given a wide berth without intrusion so the healing could take place. She threw herself into her work with maddening enthusiasm, the Payne Agency prospering by her therapeutic efforts. Expanding her agency should have provided China with that old thrill she'd felt when first putting her talent stable together. It will, she told herself. Tomorrow, when the architect laid out the plans, she'd find that excitement again.

China worked in relative silence for the rest of the afternoon, refusing most phone calls. "Look what I've got," Marce said, barging back in and tossing a thick contract on her desk. At least China's grimace was a shade of her old self, Marce thought. "Have fun."

"Hold on a second," China called, dropping her eyes to

the stack of dreaded papers. "Phone Mandy Temple and let her know she won the role of the governor's mistress. Tell her that I'll get her the best possible contract, and as soon as legal has made mumbo-jumbo of it, we'll make an appointment for her to come in."

"But . . . but, China," Marce stuttered. "You always make those calls. Are you sure you don't want to do it yourself?"

Blunt, gray eyes rose from their study of the typed papers. "I'm sure."

Marce moved deeper into the teal and alabaster room. And for the first time ever China saw anger storm across the young girl's face. "This I'm-dead-but-still-walking-around routine doesn't have anything to do with your mother tearing up that restaurant, does it? It's Reeve Laughlin. The man hasn't called here in almost two weeks."

A slight shudder escaped China before she was able to steel herself against it. Hearing Reeve's name said out loud was more painful than thinking it. Speaking it was impossible. "When are you scheduled to take your test to become a licensed agent?"

With a sigh of resigned defeat Marce said, "In two months."

"Well, you've been doing the drudgery of an agent's work for almost two years. So go on out there and see how nice it is to tell a client she's just made it to the big time."

Blessedly alone, China slumped in her chair like a boneless rag doll. She had stopped expecting Reeve to call days ago. Not because of the time that had passed, but because her instincts, which had become agonizingly accurate, insisted he had meant every word spoken that night.

What kept her from accepting his marriage proposal were the words he hadn't said—*forever, till death do us part*—as much as the words he had said. *We can try it.* Give it a whirl and not worry about the commitments and promises they might break, or China's heart. He had placed more emphasis on his boss's displeasure with yet another piece of questionable publicity. It wouldn't be the first time an up-and-coming had taken a wife to prove he was down-to-earth. He had backed off for good at the mention of children, twisting her desire for a family into an accusation.

She tried to obliterate her heartache with anger, comparing his refusal to see her again to that of a business foe shutting down all negotiations without a contract. She tried formulating a counteroffer so irresistible, he'd be lured back. She tried telling herself that time would erase his name from her heart as it had Paul's. But nothing eased the constriction in her chest, the cold fist of pain that stayed with her. A blanket seemed to have come down and smothered her will to go on without him.

Why did he get to make all the rules?

Without lifting the receiver, she toyed with the phone, punching out Reeve's number. Could she call him? Hear his voice? Have that deep baritone wrap itself around her like a warm blanket while he coldly rebuffed her?

Was he in as much pain as she? Or had he simply washed his hands of her?

"Oh, Reeve, why did you do this to us?"

"Stupid plant. What did you die for?" For lack of care, the crinkle of brown leaves seemed to accuse. "Couldn't you have held out a little longer? I'd have noticed eventually." If I don't shrivel up and waste away too.

China worked the suspended plant free of its hook and disposed of it. That was the last of them; they had all died.

She hadn't yet turned on the lights in her apartment. Evening's descent was a gray silk scarf drifting over her building to shroud her windows. A thin powder of dust lay on all the slick sharp-edged surfaces inside. There wasn't a thing to eat in the refrigerator. It occurred to China that, except for the clothes in the closet, it was as hollow and neglected as any vacant home could be.

Call him, China. She hadn't seen Reeve in over a month, and it didn't get better or easier. Only worse. *She wouldn't have children.* But she'd have Reeve, and she sure as hell wasn't going to have children without him. Other couples adjusted—those who wanted a family and for medical reasons couldn't have them.

Call him. What if it didn't last? The thought of another divorce was unbearable. Worse than this day-after-day agony?

Call him. He has scars, too, China realized. Some of them are hard to live with, especially when that coldness seeps into his eyes and he cruelly cuts people off. I can live with that. God knows I can't live without *him.*

She had just reached for the phone when it rang. It pierced the silent gloom shrilly and China nearly jumped out of her skin. Reeve was so clear in her mind, she automatically visualized him at the other end of the line. Wild hope accelerated her heartbeat to a crazy gallop. Was he lonely and unable to sleep? Did he need her next to him in his great big bed? She was so sure it would be his gritty voice that the soft feminine "Hello" left her momentarily speechless.

"China? Did I wake you?"

"Uh . . . Miriam? Is that you? No, you didn't wake me."

"Honey." The word wavered, and China gripped the edge of the sink. "China, your father . . . your father has had a heart attack." Then muffled sobs.

"Is he . . . is—"

"At the hospital. But come, China. Please hurry."

China listened to the rhythm of the machinery, all of her energy focused on detecting an irregular beep or hum. There was more natural color in Arthur Payne's face today. Someone had thought to comb his silvery hair and shave his stubble of beard. Absurd, how grateful China felt toward the anonymous person who'd remembered her father was still a human being with pride. She held his hand and watched him sleep. He had roused, Miriam said, had even talked to his doctors.

Her eyelids fell heavily. Just for a minute, she told herself, a little respite to ease the burning, scratchy grit.

Three days. Seventy-two horrendous hours. Most of them spent in the waiting room so that Miriam could be with Arthur. Not eating. Not sleeping. Waiting. And working through her guilt for not calling or visiting him recently. For harboring resentments because he hadn't lived up to an image of China's own making.

And remembering.

He'd taught her to ride a bike in Central Park, letting go of the back fender when he had promised he wouldn't. She'd pumped that two-wheeler for yards before realizing she was on her own. Instead of pride in her accomplishment, she'd been furious, near tears of fright because he had let go when he had promised not to. "But you did just fine on your own, China. You didn't need me after all."

China held more tightly to her father's hand; so tightly, her own hand cramped.

"Chippy, let go of my hand, or next they'll be setting broken bones."

"Daddy," she breathed. "Oh, Dad." She bit down on her lower lip to prevent a rush of tears.

"Now, don't cry, China. I'm going to be all right."

"I thought I had lost you."

"Not while you've got this grip on me. You planning on playing tug-of-war with God?"

Uncontrollably the tears fell. But between the wet paths streaking her cheeks, her full lips curved into a smile of utter relief. "They're going to move you to Progressive Care soon."

The pair of eyes that sharpened with anxiety were, surprisingly, Arthur Payne's. "We've both been to hell and back, haven't we?" Her gaze shifted away to fix on the speckled tile floor. "I read the papers, China. Clare is—"

"Just fine." China had no intention of letting her mother's lunacy have the far-reaching effects of giving her father another heart attack. "She and Martin just returned from a second honeymoon. And Joey, you remember Joey, don't you, Dad?"

"Mmm. Nice boy."

"Very. He isn't going back to military school. He's going to live with Clare and Martin here in New York, be a regular family."

"You don't mind that? Seems I remember you insisting the boy *not* live with Clare—"

"Joey is her son, not mine," China said firmly. "Now, no more talking. They'll kick me out of here if you overdo."

"Then I'm going to stand up on this bed and make a speech. You need to be kicked out of here. You look like hell, sweetheart." His eyes lovingly touched her face. "Go on home, China. Have a life—I'm going to."

She leaned over her father and kissed his forehead. He smiled up at her. "Go home, honey."

"I love you, Dad."

She went out into the hall and headed for the elevators. Her strung-out nerves began to let go with the force of piano wires pinging free. Her father would live, the waiting was over, and she was going home. Without her anxiety for fuel the nervous energy that had kept her going for the last seventy-two hours seeped out of her. The gentle hum of the elevator falling to ground level nearly put her out completely. A shocking burst of cold air when she stepped outside revived her enough to find a taxi and give the cabby the address. She lay back on the seat, seeing the neighborhoods pass in an unfocused blur.

She was going home. Finally.

Thirteen

China wrestled with the heavy, cagelike doors, nearly losing the battle in her fatigue. As the freight elevator clanged and creaked up three floors she wondered if Reeve could hear the racket. She had her answer when the big room stopped and she saw him, hands on hips and head cocked to one side in curiosity. A soul-parching thirst was slaked when her eyes licked over his face, and she understood why the recovered alcoholic could never again taste the habit-forming nectar without wanting to drown in it. A tight coil in her midsection snapped loose; electrifying vibrations raced along her nerves, further weakening her limbs.

"China?" His eyes filled with concern as he slid the metal doors open. The clothes she had sat, paced, and slept in for three days were given a once-over from beneath his furrowed brow. "Come in, China."

She felt herself begin to sway. "We may have to do this the hard way."

He caught her in his arms as her legs gave out. The tender possession of his strong arms was her final undoing. She didn't need to wrap her arms around him; he wouldn't drop her.

"What in God's name has happened?" he demanded, setting her down in a cushioned easy chair and crouching on his heels in front of her. His eyes tore over her, frightened at the sight of her bleached complexion, glazed eyes, and sagging shoulders.

"Oh, thank you, Reeve. This chair is so soft. Hospitals have the worst chairs—"

"Hospitals!" He claimed her chin between his fingers to get a better look at her. "You've been in the hospital? You're hurt? Dammit, China, tell me what happened to you!"

"No. My father." She let her head sink a little into the support of his hand, her cheek resting in his warm palm. "A heart attack." The thick black lashes framing his startled blue eyes kept blurring out of focus to charcoal smudges. "Three days ago."

"I'm sorry. I know you loved him." He let go of her chin and her head sagged tiredly. "So you've come here to hide and heal. Close out reality? I'm still good enough for that, huh?"

He was angry. That was good, China decided. Cold and detached would have been too great a barrier for her to penetrate. Indifference might very well have killed her. But angry was good. Happy would have been better.

"He didn't die, Reeve. He's okay. I'm okay."

"You're not okay."

She wanted to explain that she hadn't come in defeat and despair. She didn't want to be his queen needing him as her knight charging to her defense. But coherent thoughts wouldn't formulate. The little compartments in her brain were shutting down one by one. "I'm just so tired, Reeve."

He stood up and took a step back. "Haven't you slept at all?" She shook her head, seeing the soft-worn denim wrapping his slim hips.

"Have you eaten anything in the last three days?" Again she could only shake her head. The instinct to put her arms around his lean thighs and let her head fall against his muscled hips was so strong, she swayed in her seat. Her dull gaze traveled up to his face. He was glaring down at her, and she wondered with vague curiosity why Reeve looked as battle-weary as she felt.

"Now, that wasn't very sensible." He bent down and began unbuttoning her jacket. China thought she heard emotion color his gruff voice, but she couldn't be sure of anything that demanded brain power. "What's happened to my sensible, practical China?"

"Am I still your China?" With her eyes shut she smiled. "Maybe I've lost my sensible, practical mind. Wouldn't that be nice?" If he answered her, she didn't hear it as a black void opened up to claim her.

A cool draft brushed her arms and back, and China tried to snuggle up to the shifting warmth at her breasts. Her shivers and the irritating jolts to her body as someone moved her around wrenched her out of the weightless world she had been floating in. She was standing up, or trying to. As she dragged her heavy eyelids open, the loft swam fuzzily before her, a kaleidoscope of wood and brass and bright paints.

"Home," she said with a yawn. "I'm home." She gazed down at the top of Reeve's head bent to the task of undressing her. "Never miss an opportunity, do you?" she mumbled happily.

His thumbs fumbled with her bra before unpuzzling the hooks. "I've run a hot tub. After your bath I'm putting you to bed. You might as well go back to sleep, you're in no condition to be of any help."

Her head thumped down to his shoulder. As he bent to

slide her slacks down her legs she drooped along like a rag doll. Unsteadily balancing their combined weight to keep them both from falling, Reeve hauled China back to a standing position. "I can't do it with your legs bent, honey."

"Sure you can. You always do it with my legs bent." She buried her nose in his shirt collar, giving in to a fit of giggles. She felt silly—uncontrollably slaphappy.

"Sounds like you tried a couple hits of ether," Reeve muttered. "Now, keep your legs straight. Lock your knees."

"Aye, aye, sir." China raised her hand in salute and stiffened her long, half-naked body to weave like a boat mast on a windy day. With one arm around her waist to steady her Reeve finally worked the rest of her clothes off. He felt so good. So close. "Keep holding me like this, Reeve. I'm so tired . . . I missed you so. God, is the room spinning for you too?"

He swung her up into his arms and strode into the steamed-up bathroom. "It's called fatigue, sweetheart. You're suffering from seventy-two hours of physical exhaustion."

"That should go nicely with my nervous breakdown!"

Eased into the hot water, China felt her heated blood course through her veins. Her brain turned as soggy and limp as her muscles, sedated into floating lethargy. Reeve rolled up his sleeves and knelt at the side of the claw-footed tub, supporting her head as his soapy hands moved over her. China sighed and closed her eyes. The weight of her breast was cuddled in a slippery palm, the nipple peaking in anticipation of his rough fingertip. Reeve's soothing, coaxing, ministering hands seemed to be everywhere; the back of her neck, making delicious circles on her stomach, skating across her ribs, massaging behind her knees. Her senses could hardly absorb the thrilling messages of his gliding fingers before they moved on.

"You won't believe this," China murmured, her head rolling on his shoulder until her lips touched the corded muscle in his throat. "But I'm going to fall asleep again."

She floated upward into perfect stillness. Moonlight washed in through the window wall, laying opal squares on the golden floor. Bright red embers were glowing from a bank of ashes in the fireplace. China lay flat on her back in bed, a heavy, curled arm hooked to her waist. She was, she realized, naked under the sheet and quilt. And her body was heavy with the ache of having been brought to the edge of physical awareness and left there. Inching onto her side so as not to wake Reeve, she rolled her head until her face was a breath away from his. Sapphire eyes glittered through the shadows at her.

"Someone's been sleeping in my bed," she said in a tiny whisper. "And there he is."

"I was going to ask how you're feeling. I see I don't have to."

"I feel fantastic. You wouldn't think just a couple hours sleep could make such a difference." The security of his embrace encouraged her hands to seek his furred chest, her fingers sinking into the pelt of crisp black hair.

"You've been out cold for twenty-one hours."

"God! No wonder I'm so hungry." She reached out with one hand to trace his jaw and chiseled lips while the fingers of her other hand explored his sprawled nudity under the covers with slow deliberateness.

He grew rigid and moved away. "I'll scare something up in the kitchen."

"I've already got what I want." She held him in such a way, he didn't dare move another inch. An angry muscle stood out on the underside of his jaw. Moonlight flashed on the brace and release of his teeth, which were clenched beneath the taut skin. Even as he pulsed to passionate life beneath her hands, he withdrew emotionally.

"Why did you come here, China?"

"To touch you. To make love with you."

"I think it's a little early in your recovery for rigorous exercise." His tone of voice was chilling, and the instruction for hands-off clear.

But she'd been too many nights without him not to have him now, this instant. She had slept in his bed so long, the musky, male scent of him permeating the pillowcase had become part of the very air she breathed.

"And I think this is exactly what you planned." She settled herself over him, planting kisses on his throat and uncovered shoulders, her breasts crushed to his chest. "Otherwise I would have been modestly wrapped in one of your shirts and you . . . well, you wouldn't be so deliciously naked."

She teased his lips apart with damp, moist kisses, inviting his tongue into her mouth. His heart slammed at the wall of his chest, thumping furiously on her palm. Spontaneously her hips rocked against him, moving them both on long waves of desire until the shivers running throughout him vibrated under her.

She put her lips to his ear to whisper, "If you didn't want to make love, why did I sleep naked in your arms?"

A guttural groan of frustration tore itself from between his clamped teeth. He was as fluid and fast as quicksilver, overturning China to gain the upper hand and the dominant position. He knelt above her, holding himself suspended on all fours, his hands pinning her extended arms over her head. His knees embedded themselves in the mattress, sinking with the bulk of his weight. One leg pressed to the outside of her hips while the other opened her legs, brushing the soft flesh of her inner thighs. He was a poised jungle cat, his captured prey imprisoned beneath him.

"I'm too strong for you, China. You don't stand a chance playing physical games with me."

Her smoky gray gaze traveled a route of whipcord muscles, past the wiry mat of chest hairs to the silky arrow pointing out the final prize she was after. "Oh, I don't know about that, Reeve. I'm doing pretty well so far."

"Don't try a battle of wits either."

"Are we pulling out all stops? You're at a distinct disadvantage. Your responses to my moves aren't as easy to hide as mine are from you."

"Didn't you learn anything from our chess game?"

"Mmm-hmm," she purred. "I know what the spoils are now. And that's what I'm after. The pound of flesh that goes to the winner."

His legs slid down the mattress so that he melted to her from ankles to hipbones. He held his upper body away with straight arms. She knew his desire, felt the hard thrust of him feather her stomach as he moved and then brush the sensitive flesh of her inner thigh. When Reeve saw the glow of white-hot embers flare up instantly in those ash-gray eyes, his cool smile reflected secret satisfaction.

"If you think you can hide your body's responses from me, China, then you're a fool. I know you too well; every quiver and twitch speaks to me." Without lowering his upper body, he brought his lips to her breast. His tongue circled the rigid, budding tip, then flicked the dusky velvet to a pout before hungrily nipping it between his teeth. When his mouth closed over the throbbing peak, a flash fire raced through her veins. His long, thirsty pulls fanned the flames to inferno intensity.

"Oh," she gasped with the resultant shock. She tried to clasp him to her but he refused to loosen his hold on her hands. He hovered, gazing down. "See. Loud and clear your body speaks to me." Then he proved his point with equal attention to her other breast and China's fingers curled into her palms until her nails bit at the skin.

"What's the name of this game, China?"

No more games, her heart cried. But she had started this, she was committed to seeing it through. "I don't care what the name of the game is." Her voice was low and passion-laden. "So long as we play . . . and I win."

She couldn't hold her hips still. Rhythmically she thrust toward and away from him until he had to grab at the air for breath. "Name the game, I'll play." His eyes raked over her. "We'll see who wins."

"Follow the leader. I lead."

The hard manacle of his hand on her wrists relaxed enough so that she could move her arms. She gradually brought one hand down between their faces, his thumb and finger still braceleting her slender wrist. With a pointed finger she traced his full lower lip, swelled from the force of his kisses. "Do this."

He released her wrist and stared down into her face with an expression that was guarded and skeptical. Shifting his weight to one elbow, he began to copy the patterns she was tracing, each of them exploring the other's mouth, each of them nipping softly at the flesh of the other.

Next her fingers combed his tousled black hair to barely brush the back of his neck. Then she raked her nails down his back with a calculated touch, one that slammed a response through his hard body but didn't draw blood.

"Now, do that," she commanded in a hoarse, breathless voice.

Reeve's fingers tunneled through silky hair to her

scalp, dragging China's head back, exposing the creamy length of her throat. When he reached the nape of her neck, he didn't mimic her light touch, but massaged her muscles until they dissolved to fluid heat. He couldn't reach her back where it was pressed to the mattress, so he gently raked his fingernails over her slim shoulders, across the fullness of her breasts and down her side to her waist. He was profoundly better at this than she was.

Both of her hands sought the jutting crest of his hip-bones, and she pressed her thumbs to the hard ridges, making small, suggestive circles, drawing him closer. "And this."

"China . . ." He struggled with a lodged breath. "China . . ."

Her eyes were soft bottomless pools. "Come on, you can do it." She carried his hand to the luxuriantly furred mound beneath which she was liquid desire.

He arched against her, his buttocks tightening. She saw hot desire come and go in his eyes as cold anger fought to dominate his emotions. "Dammit, China. I'll take you, if you want it that badly. And then . . . who wins?"

"I do." Her words were two separate, soft pants, as fragile as the tears that slid from the corners of her eyes to dampen the hair at her temples. "No more games," she whispered, finally saying the words. "Please, Reeve, no more games."

He held himself still, watching the crystal drops slip over her petal-soft skin. "Ah, dammit." He rolled to his side, then dropped to the bed, lying on his back. "Don't! Don't cry."

China had to force each shallow breath. As she lay there watching Reeve massage his closed eyes she thought her heart might stop beating and she would die. This had never occurred to her—that Reeve didn't want her anymore. That he hadn't been as consumed by thoughts of her this past month as she had been of him. He couldn't forgive her lack of trust.

"I see." Her voice, too, was cold. She was angry now. She had come to him, ready to compromise, willing to give up children and a family to be his wife. And he—he couldn't forgive one night of cruel words. "You've cut me out of your life then. Washed your hands of me. But that's what you do best, Reeve. Isn't it?"

He lay there staring at the ceiling.

"Answer me, damn you!" A sob rose up with her fierce demand and tore from her throat. "In only a month you've wiped me out."

"I sure as hell tried." He turned his face to her, naked and raw with pain. "I've tried. But it was as impossible as cutting out my own soul. As fatal as trying to wash the blood from my body." His voice was gruff and carried tears even though his eyes remained dry. But China cried; for him, for her.

"Sh, sh." He gathered her close to his side. "Please, babe, don't. I hate for you to cry; I hate that I make you cry." He held her so tightly, his arms were painful bands, yet China relished it after the agony of empty space between them. "My mother cried. How I remember the sound of her sobs at night, all because of a man, because of Martin. And now . . . now I seem bent on doing the same to you."

China turned her face on his shoulder, tipping her chin in order to look him in the eyes. There was so much she wanted to say, but his need to unburden seemed greater and so she remained silent.

"You frustrate me, honey," Reeve continued. "Half the time I don't know whether to wrap you up in cotton and protect you, or throw you at the mercy of all you fear and hate, hoping you'll build up your own defenses." He studied the gray eyes staring into his, so wide and serious. "I'm sorry, hon, for those news articles. I knew what it did to you and I kept on planting them. You asked me not to bring Martin back. You asked me not to represent Clare—"

China put her fingertips to his lips to quiet him. Enough. She understood now why he had looked so haggard when she had first arrived, the source of the lines that still etched his face. "I know," China said softly. "Me too. The more I fell in love with you, the harder I fought it. Until finally when you asked me to marry you, I did something that would send you away forever. I said no."

"But why, China?" His arms had relaxed as they were talking, and she sought the warmth of his skin with her fingers as tentatively as she sought the answer to his question. "I was committed to you by then. A hundred percent."

"I wasn't ready to give everything yet. Can you understand that you just got there first?"

"Are you saying you're ready now, China?"

"Oh, Reeve. I realized the moment I had to live without you that you'd had all of me for a long time. So much of my heart, my love. I can't face another day without you."

He crushed her to his chest, tangled his legs with hers, combed his hands through her hair. With his lips pressed to her throat, he pledged his love over and over again.

"I need you, Reeve. Not insurance or promises, just you." She cradled the head that lay on her breast now, feeling strong and necessary to the man who lay beside her.

"A marriage vow *is* a promise, China. Till death do us part. Let no man put asunder. Forever."

They came together then, each of them moving toward the other, neither the winner or loser. The joining of their bodies was a sweet, loving, trusting union.

China had replenished her body in order of its own demands. With sleep. With Reeve. Now she was famished. Reeve, reading that hungry glint in her eye, rose from the bed and walked, unashamed of his nudity, to the kitchen. "What shall it be?" he called out to her. "A feast or just fast?"

"Fast, I think." China stood and stretched lazily. The morning sun, creeping over the rooftops, flooded the loft with the uncertain blush of a beginning day. As the loft accepted the light China looked around it with new eyes, those of one looking at her home for the first time. She saw an oil painting, a new one, propped against a wall, and curled up on the fur rug in front of it to enjoy the bright, beautiful colors. She recognized the style as being that of a SoHo artist Reeve had once taken her to meet. The woman's name in the left-hand corner confirmed it.

The artist had skillfully captured a sunny, country picnic with a camera's eye for detail, evoking the sweet smell of damp grass and wind-bent flowers. China gazed with interest at the three generations represented. A dark-haired woman was in the foreground, her busy hands setting food out on a table spread with a checkered cloth. Grandma rocked a swaddled baby under a spreading maple tree while Grandpa looked on. In the distance a father and son played ball while another young boy fished at a stream. The brass plaque mounted in the center of the frame bore the title of the work: *Family*.

The mood was radically different from anything Reeve had purchased previously, but China liked it. She glanced up at the walls across the room, wondering where it should go. It didn't seem to fit at all. An incredible warmth was depicted in this painting, but it was the attention to detail that would be lost to the viewer unless the picture had an honored place of its own.

She curled her knees to her breasts, once again gazing at the painting. And then she grew perfectly still as her eyes focused on first one then another face in the country scene.

Was her imagination playing tricks on her? Was it just some unbelievable coincidence? She lifted her finger to the little boy, arm curved behind him, theatrically positioned to pitch the ball. She could swear that little boy had the most uncanny resemblance to Reeve.

"Oh," she gasped. It was them. All of them. Clare and Martin, years from now, with white hair and frail bodies. At a far-off stream Joey was fishing. China was setting the table. Reeve and a son, their son. . . . The oil dabs blurred as tears filled her eyes and emotion flooded her heart. She touched the tiny face of that small boy at the same moment that Reeve folded his body to hers on the floor, his warm chest pressed to her back.

"Every little boy I see," he whispered at her ear. "For weeks now. I can't pass by a little boy without seeing my face. Or it's little girls with big gray eyes and long coltish legs. I had this done for you. I tried to send it over, but each day it came back. You've been with your father all the time. I thought you were refusing me."

China turned her face to meet his gaze, tears streaming down her cheeks. Warm, glistening tears that Reeve let slip onto his fingers, knowing them to be tears of joy. "Children, Reeve? Our children?"

"Hundreds if you want." He gently kissed her cheeks, drying the wet paths with his lips. "Laughlin sons and daughters. The world will know China and Reeve were here."

Her heart galloped in her chest. She didn't know such happiness existed. "The world already knows we're here!"

China lay back on the fur rug, twining her arms around Reeve's neck and pulling him down on top of her. "Can you just imagine the write-up the christening will get? We'll have to start a scrapbook for the kids."

"You mean, you're going to start saving those damn articles?" His voice was too breathless to have an angry edge as his flesh met and connected with hers.

"Not your average scrapbook."

"We're not your average family."

"Family," China breathed out in awesome wonder. "Give me a baby, Reeve. My body craves all the life you can bring it."

"Shouldn't we get married first?" Yet he was already marveling at how quickly her soft curves could bring him to hard desire.

"Tomorrow we'll get married. Today we'll get pregnant."

There was little he could do to prevent his body's response to China's ministrations. Nor did he want to. "Calling all the shots, aren't you?" he complained, even as fresh passion bathed his face.

"Oh, Mr. Laughlin," China whispered at his ear. "You ain't seen nothin' yet."

Moments later the sun cleared the tallest New York skyscraper and burst into the loft in golden glory as a bright new day was born.

THE EDITOR'S CORNER

Please be sure to turn to the back of this book for a special treat—an excerpt from the novel **CHASE THE MOON** by a marvelous British author, Catherine Nicolson. I hope the short sample of this extraordinarily romantic story will prompt you to ask your bookseller for the book next month when you get your four LOVESWEPTs. And, of course, we believe those four LOVESWEPTs are real treats, too!

It astonishes me at times how our authors continue to top themselves book after book. They're all talented authors who are devoted to expanding their imaginations and developing the skills of their craft. And I know how hard they work. Still, I'm often surprised at the high level of creativity they are able to maintain. And no author demonstrates better those qualities of originality and ingenuity in superb romantic storytelling than Kay Hooper.

IF THERE BE DRAGONS, LOVESWEPT #71, is one of Kay's most emotionally touching romances. The surprises you expect from a Kay Hooper book are abundant in this story of lovely Brooke Kennedy whose rare gift has kept her a virtual prisoner of loneliness. But, thanks to that delightful meddler Pepper, a golden knight comes to her rescue. Cody Nash, Thor's best friend in **PEPPER'S WAY,** enters Brooke's world and brings her the warmth and light of love. I'll never forget Brooke and her dragons, Cody and his virile tenderness . . . or a very special "wild" creature who contributes a unique and heartwarming dimension to this wonderful story.

(continued)

Sandra Kleinschmit makes her debut as a published author next month with a nifty romance, **PROBABLE CAUSE**, LOVESWEPT #72. Jami Simpson isn't playing cops and robbers when she detains a man she suspects of breaking and entering. She's a police officer all right, but Lance Morgan is hardly a burglar . . . or is he? He assaults Jami's emotions and tries to steal her heart in a love story that's sensitive and fun. We hope you'll join us in giving this brand new author the warmly enthusiastic welcome you've given the other talented writers we've been so pleased to be able to publish for the first time.

And speaking of new talents, here comes BJ James again with **MORE THAN FRIENDS**, LOVESWEPT #73. BJ's first book, **WHEN YOU SPEAK LOVE**, was vibrant with dramatic tension, though touched with humor; her second romance shows her versatility in a work that's full of charming lightheartedness, though touched with dramatic tension. The heroine of **MORE THAN FRIENDS** is pocket-sized Jamie, the sister of six brawny males. She's grown up in a household devoted to competitive sports and has always been in the thick of rough and tumble football games and fierce races, never asking for privilege because of her sex or size. Then she literally tackles a gentle giant named Mike Bradford and he tries to turn her life around. You'll be as appalled—and impressed—as Mike is by Jamie's foolish physical courage . . . and her confusion about the conflict between competition and independence. What a love story!

Ah, it is such a delight for me to tell you about **CHARADE**, LOVESWEPT #74, by Joan Elliott Pickart. This sensual love story is spiked by some of the most amusing exchanges it's been my pleasure to read. (One line in particular struck me as so side-splittingly funny that my son ran into the room where I was reading to see if I was choking!) **CHARADE,** as the title suggests, is a merry romance in which heroine Whitney assumes a false identity . . . and gets trapped (hmm, quite deliciously) in her role by one of the most captivating of all possible heroes. The marvelous cast of secondary characters—from a soap opera heart-throb to a babbling would-be vamp—truly enrich this tale. Watch out for the hero's dear old gray-haired Aunt Olive. She has a surprise or two up her sleeve!

Enjoy! And do continue to write to us. Your comments are so helpful and so interesting!

Warm good wishes,
Sincerely,

Carolyn Nichols

Carolyn Nichols
    Editor
LOVESWEPT
Bantam Books, Inc.
666 Fifth Avenue
New York, NY 10103

Dear LOVESWEPT reader:

CHASE THE MOON is a one-in-a-million book, the kind of story that won't let you rest until you've finished it, and then won't fade from your heart and mind for months. Set apart from other novels in the romance genre by its unusual blend of the richly exotic and the touchingly innocent, CHASE THE MOON is a fairy tale for grown-ups, created of mystery and magic, beauty and sensuality, fantasy and fulfillment. And next month it will be available from your bookseller.

The heroine's name is Corrie Modena, alias Columbine. A naive, lonely orphan whose stunning musical talent drives her in search of fame and fortune, she has confided her secret dreams to only one man—an enigmatic stranger she knows only through letters signed Harlequin. Although they have never met, theirs is a perfect, trusting love . . . until the night that Corrie meets Guy de Chardonnet at the opera. The magnetic attraction that Corrie and Guy feel is immediate and fierce, although they are constantly at odds with each other. But Corrie is torn between Guy and her burning ambition, an ambition that Harlequin, in his letters, urges her not to betray. Corrie determines to leave Guy, realizing that Harlequin is right—for how can she know that the man to whom she's lost her heart is the steadfast keeper of her soul?

The storyline is magical, but what makes CHASE THE MOON truly unique is the extraordinary way in which the story is told. The writing is exquisitely sensual, skillfully evoking the sights, smells, tactile experiences, tastes, and sounds of the world Corrie and Guy share—a world of light: an apricot moon hanging in the still azure sky above the Riviera; sunlight; stage lighting; the dazzling spangles and sequins refracting light on costumes; the play of shadow and moonlight spilling into the nighttime ocean. Even Corrie's voice is described as having the deep and dark quality of "L'heure bleue," the strange blue hour between summer twilight and summer night. Dusky, fragrant, and everchanging, the world of CHASE THE MOON is memorable and magical, even to its elusive characters: the "real" Guy and Corrie, the fantasy Harlequin and Columbine. And CHASE THE MOON could perhaps only have been written by Catherine Nicolson—a lovely woman from Great Britain who possesses abundant charm and talent.

CHASE THE MOON is spellbinding . . . a world of romantic fantasies come breathtakingly true—where two lovers have no secrets from each other . . . except their names. It was a special delight for me to be Catherine's editor on this book. I hope the excerpt on the following pages will captivate you so much that you'll be sure to ask your bookseller for CHASE THE MOON.

Carolyn Nichols

Chase the Moon

by Catherine Nicolson

He had invited her to Paradise to enjoy oysters and peacocks . . . and she'd been unable to resist.

She turned, slowly. He looked different, younger. Against the white of his suit his skin was lightly tanned, with a satiny evenness that disturbed her. His hair, touched by the late sun, had reddish hints. Only his ice-gray eyes were unchanged. She felt suddenly confused. Perhaps in these few short weeks he had grown younger and she had grown older, perhaps they were growing together, like herself and the Balenciaga . . . She halted the thought. It didn't make sense.

"You don't seem surprised." She spoke abruptly to hide her confusion.

"Should I be?" He smiled at her, a lazy, self-assured, mocking smile.

"I might not have come."

His smile deepened, touched his eyes briefly.

"I knew you would come. You wouldn't be able to resist it. The oysters or the peacocks would persuade you, one or the other. And curiosity. All women like the same things."

"Really?" She spoke with some asperity. She was not and would never be like all women. "What might those things be?"

He smiled down at her lazily, shrugged.

"Silk. Paris. Compliments. Surprises." He offered her his arm. "Besides . . ." His tone was gently conversational. "I always get what I want."

"Always?" She was uneasily aware of the warmth of his skin through the soft material of his sleeve.

"Almost always."

Ceremoniously he escorted her back to the table overlooking the garden. She felt strange, as if she were in a dream. The restaurant was still deserted, they had the whole gallery room to themselves. It made her feel unreal, timeless, as if they were both on a stage, acting out a kind of play for an unseen audience. A waiter materialized out of the wings. She noticed for the first time that there was no menu.

Guy nodded in response to the waiter's inquiring glance. Not a word was spoken. The waiter disappeared as silently as a fish.

"I hope you're hungry." She was conscious of his eyes on her face.

"I'm always hungry."

"I know, I remember." He smiled. She felt a blush coloring her cheeks and refused to acknowledge it. The past meant nothing, she could rise above it.

"And you . . . Are you always late?"

"Touché." He spoke mildly, offering neither explanations nor excuses. She felt a fleeting tinge of admiration. His effrontery rivaled her own, though she had to admit his had a degree more style.

The waiter reappeared, with a large tray in his arms. As he set it down carefully Corrie saw to her astonishment that it was filled from edge to edge with small shallow bowls, each containing what seemed like no more than a mouthful of different dishes. Guy dismissed the waiter with a nod of approval. Corrie stared at the table. There was scarcely a spare inch of tablecloth to be seen.

"What is this?" She looked up to find Guy studying her with that annoying hint of irony.

"You told me you wanted everything. Well, here it is. Something from every single dish on the Belvedere's not inextensive menu." Her eyes widened. "There's more to come, but there wasn't enough room on the table." His smile was limpidly ingenuous. "Eat up, or it will get cold." He handed her a small silver dish. "I suggest you begin with the smoked oysters."

The unmistakable challenge in his eyes was irresistible. Corrie instantly resolved to do justice to the feast or die in the attempt. She'd show him what it meant to be hungry.

Manfully, she set to work. He watched in growing astonishment as she polished off dish after dish, chasing the last drops of sauce with catlike delicacy. Lobster bisque and *consommé madrilène, chateaubriand printanier, suprême* of sole, artichoke hearts, soft carps' roe, lamb cutlets, veal escalopes with apples and cream, flamed in calvados, crab claws dressed in pistachio nut oil. Invisibly the empty dishes were whisked away to be replenished with tiny spring vegetables, duckling with green pepper and brandy sauce, wild strawberries, brandied peaches, chicken stuffed with braised fennel roots, shrimp soufflé . . . Recklessly she mixed sweet with savory, fish with fowl, red meat with white. It was a cornucopia of delights, a Roman orgy. White Burgundy followed red, Nuits St. Georges chasing Pouilly Fuissé, and capped with a rainbow assortment of different ice creams.

"Are you quite sure you've had enough?" His tone was elaborately solicitous as she pushed away the last ice-cream dish and patted her lips with a napkin. She nodded, so full she could barely speak.

"Yes, I think so." She glimpsed a remaining petit four and downed it with relish. "For the moment."

He shook his head in mock astonishment. "You'll be sick."

"I'm never sick. I have the digestion of a camel."

"So I see. How do you manage it?"

"It's quite simple. All you have to do is eat with your spine." She took a deep breath. "And there's something else."

"What's that?" He was regarding her with as much polite interest as he would have shown a real camel in a zoo.

"Motivation."

"Motivation?" He frowned, puzzled.

"Perhaps you've never heard of it." She allowed a slight trace of sarcasm to enter her tone. "It's called hunger."

"Indeed." He seemed unmoved, just faintly curious. "You interest me, Miss Modena. Why should a woman in your position . . ." his eyes rested lazily on her bare shoulders—"ever have to suffer such an indignity? Surely your patron cannot be such an ogre? Or is it . . ." Here his eyes took on a mocking gleam. "Can it possibly be that he prefers slender women?"

Corrie drew herself to her full height and with an heroic effort choked back her anger at the implied insult.

"M. de Chardonnet." She spoke with dignity, as befitted a widow recently bereaved. "I no longer have a patron."

"Oh." He seemed surprised, even concerned. She gritted her teeth, disguised her fury behind demurely cast down eyes. Doubtless he couldn't imagine how a young woman could survive without the support and protection of a man such as himself. "Are you no longer at the Savoy?"

"From tomorrow, no." She thought about coaxing a tear, decided against it. She was bereaved, but brave.

"Because of me?"

The effrontery of the man! He didn't seem in the least abashed—if anything he sounded pleased, almost gratified. He assumed, of course, that she'd been dismissed by her patron because of one evening spent in another man's company. Such arrogance . . .

"You could say so." She sighed deeply.

"My deepest sympathy." He was smiling a small, knowing smile, as if now at last he had her in his power.

"I don't want your sympathy, thank you very much!" A trace of tartness entered her tone. His smile broadened.

"Perhaps another petit four?"

"Certainly not." She folded her hands primly in her lap. He was still looking at her with that disturbing, assessing gaze. He gestured at the waiter to clear away the remaining dishes.

"At least you enjoyed your meal."

The touch of irony in his voice brought a blush to her cheeks. A healthy appetite hardly became the grieving widow . . . But it was too late now.

"It was delicious." Belatedly she remembered her manners. "Thank you." A thought struck her suddenly; she frowned in puzzlement. "But why has no one else come to eat here? They don't know what they're missing."

He smiled patiently.

"Because I've engaged the entire restaurant."

"What?"

Now he really had managed to surprise her. "Just for us?" It was an extraordinary extravagance, it almost made her feel ill.

"Of course."

"Do you mean . . . they've cooked all these different dishes . . . just for me?"

"Of course."

"You mean, there's a whole rack of lamb back there, and I've just had one mouthful?"

"I've no idea. I should imagine so. It hadn't occurred to me."

He smiled indulgently. "I could ask for it to be put in a bag for you, if you like. We could take it with us."

She leaned back in her chair, half amused, half appalled. He and she were worlds apart. She couldn't even begin to imagine what it must be like to live as he did, to spend as if money were a mere toy for his own amusement. And yet he himself had barely touched a mouthful of the feast.

"Why didn't you eat anything?"

He shrugged. "As you say, it is a question of . . . motivation. I preferred to watch you."

She blushed again. It hadn't been the sort of performance she'd intended. She stared at him. The light from the gardens outside was deepening infinitesimally into blue, flattering, softening, making outlines unreal.

"Now, Mademoiselle Corrie, you have done ample justice to the oysters. It is time for peacocks."

In a dream she took his proffered arm. She could no longer remember whether she liked him or not, she was too full of good food for logic. As they emerged into the air she saw there were no other people in sight. A thought struck her.

"You haven't hired the whole of the park as well?"

"No." He laughed, the deep spontaneous laugh which she was beginning to like, to try and prize out of him. Slowly they walked up toward the ornamental garden. Around them she felt the faintest stir of breeze, bringing with it the hypnotic scent of newly mown grass. Sunlight glinted off the little clocktower with its turquoise copper roof and golden ball. The old rose bricks of the arcade leading to the orangery were soft in the sunlight, the shadows violet beneath the murmuring trees. He was right. It was as near as man could get to Paradise.

Beneath the trees, in the emerald green shade where the grass bloomed with an underwater intensity, rabbits browsed while on the high old walls peacocks strutted and bowed, saluting the evening with their harsh haunting cries. Everything around them was poised timelessly on the brink of summer, every rabbit soft and fat with plenty, every peacock with its hen.

Against her will, she was drawn into the fairy-tale. She couldn't resist the peacocks. Their voices had the authority, the aching, soulful penetration of a prima donna soprano. Those slender necks and tiny heads didn't look capable of producing such a noise. And they moved so slowly, sure of their charisma, milking their audience. The last light was brilliant on their opalescent plumage. How much she wanted to be a peacock.

They halted, mesmerized. A peacock eyed them motionlessly with its malachite gaze. His snake-like neck, insufferably blue, waved, searching, swelling. He emitted a superb, spine-shaking shriek. And then slowly, like a magician, he produced his tail, spreading it like a moonscape, a heaven full of dancing planets. He stayed there, quivering for enough time to stun them, then shuffled his feathers back with a businesslike air, squawked once and stalked away.

It was a revelation. They looked at each other with a sort of awe. They had been privileged, it was as if royalty had stopped to speak to them in the street. They had shared something irreplaceable, unrepeatable.

"What was that?" Her voice was a whisper. She hardly dared to break the silence, but she wanted to spread her own plumes for him, tell him her plans and dreams, flaunt her secret inner world.

"Serendipity." He turned to her, his white suit dappled under the shimmering leaves. "I never realized . . ." His voice was soft, like someone woken from a deep sleep. "Your eyes are so blue, violet, actually."

They stared at each other. The image of the peacock's tail still seemed to be imprinted on her retina, a dazzling mist of color. She couldn't see, couldn't think.

"Come with me." His voice was low. "Come with me to Paris. Now, tonight."

Paris, Paris, Paradise . . . It sounded so easy. It would be easy. She could float away and never be heard of again, supported by him and his money, like a swimmer in the Dead Sea. But it wasn't enough, it couldn't be enough for her.

She shook her head. The peacock's plumes were fading, the moment was lost. She couldn't go to Paris with a man who'd only just noticed the color of her eyes.

Dear Harlequin,

What's happening to me? Why can't I stop thinking about him? He's nothing special, just a collection of cells and corpuscles like me, and yet I think if I saw him in the street I'd throw away everything, all the future we've planned, just to hear his voice again . . . Does that sound crazy? I wish I knew how long this was going to last. Some days I think I'm cured, I hardly think about him at all, and then at night he comes alive again as soon as I fall asleep, and I wake up crying.

I was such a fool, I don't know how I came to fall in love with him of all people. You know how I feel about rich men—surely I should have been immune?

Please, tell me I've done the right thing.

Columbine

A Towering, Romantic Saga by the Author of
LOVE'S WILDEST FIRES

HEARTS
OF
FIRE

by Christina Savage

For Cassie Tryon, Independence Day, 1776, signals a different kind of upheaval—the wild, unstoppable rebellion of her heart. For on this day, she will meet a stranger—a legendary privateer disguised in clerk's clothes, a mysterious man come to do secret, patriot's business with her father . . . a man so compelling that she knows her life will never be the same for that meeting. He is Lucas Jericho—outlaw, rebel, avenger of his family's fate at British hands, a man who is dangerous to love . . . and impossible to forget.

Buy HEARTS OF FIRE, on sale November 1, 1984, wherever Bantam paperbacks are sold, or use the handy coupon below for ordering:

#1 HEAVEN'S PRICE
By Sandra Brown
Blair Simpson had enclosed herself in the fortress of her dancing, but Sean Garrett was determined to love her anyway. In his arms she came to understand the emotions behind her dancing. But could she afford the high price of love?

#2 SURRENDER
By Helen Mittermeyer
Derry had been pirated from the church by her ex-husband, from under the nose of the man she was to marry. She remembered every detail that had driven them apart—and the passion that had drawn her to him. The unresolved problems between them grew . . . but their desire swept them toward surrender.

#3 THE JOINING STONE
By Noelle Berry McCue
Anger and desire warred within her, but Tara Burns was determined not to let Damon Mallory know her feelings. When he'd walked out of their marriage, she'd been hurt.

Damon had violated a sacred trust, yet her passion for him was as breathtaking as the Grand Canyon.

#4 SILVER MIRACLES
By Fayrene Preston
Silver-haired Chase Colfax stood in the Texas moonlight, then took Trinity Ann Warrenton into his arms. Overcome by her own needs, yet determined to have him on her own terms, she struggled to keep from losing herself in his passion.

#5 MATCHING WITS
By Carla Neggers
From the moment they met, Ryan Davis tried to outmaneuver Abigail Lawrence. She'd met her match in the Back Bay businessman. And Ryan knew the Boston lawyer was more woman than any he'd ever encountered. Only if they vanquished their need to best the other could their love triumph.

#6 A LOVE FOR ALL TIME
By Dorothy Garlock
A car crash had left its marks on Casey Farrow's beauty. So what were Dan

Murdock's motives for pursuing her? Guilt? Pity? Casey had to choose. She could live with doubt and fear . . . or learn a lesson in love.

#7 A TRYST WITH MR. LINCOLN?
By Billie Green
When Jiggs O'Malley awakened in a strange hotel room, all she saw were the laughing eyes of stranger Matt Brady . . . all she heard were his teasing taunts about their "night together" . . . and all she remembered was nothing! They evaded the passions that intoxicated them until . . . there was nowhere to flee but into each other's arms.

#8 TEMPTATION'S STING
By Helen Conrad
Taylor Winfield likened Rachel Davidson to a Conus shell, contradictory and impenetrable. Rachel battled for independence, torn by her need for Taylor's embraces and her impassioned desire to be her own woman. Could they both succumb to the temptation of the tropi-

cal paradise and still be true to their hearts?

#9 DECEMBER 32nd . . . AND ALWAYS
By Marie Michael
Blaise Hamilton made her feel like the most desirable woman on earth. Pat opened herself to emotions she'd thought buried with her late husband. Together they were unbeatable as they worked to build the jet of her late husband's dreams. Time seemed to be running out and yet—would ALWAYS be long enough?

#10 HARD DRIVIN' MAN
By Nancy Carlson
Sabrina sensed Jacy in hot pursuit, as she maneuvered her truck around the racetrack, and recalled his arms clasping her to him. Was he only using her feelings so he could take over her trucking company? Their passion knew no limits as they raced full speed toward love.

#11 BELOVED INTRUDER
By Noelle Berry McCue
Shannon Douglas hated

Michael Brady from the moment he brought the breezes of life into her shadowy existence. Yet a specter of the past remained to torment her and threaten their future. Could he subdue the demons that haunted her, and carry her to true happiness?

#12 HUNTER'S PAYNE
By Joan J. Domning
P. Lee Payne strode into Karen Hunter's office demanding to know why she was stalking him. She was determined to interview the mysterious photographer. She uncovered his concealed emotions, but could the secrets their hearts confided protect their love, or would harsh daylight shatter their fragile alliance?

#13 TIGER LADY
By Joan J. Domning
Who *was* this mysterious lover she'd never seen who courted her on the office computer, and nicknamed her Tiger Lady? And could he compete with Larry Hart, who came to repair the computer

and stayed to short-circuit her emotions? How could she choose between poetry and passion—between soul and Hart?

#14 STORMY VOWS
By Iris Johansen
Independent Brenna Sloan wasn't strong enough to reach out for the love she needed, and Michael Donovan knew only how to take—until he met Brenna. Only after a misunderstanding nearly destroyed their happiness, did they surrender to their fiery passion.

#15 BRIEF DELIGHT
By Helen Mittermeyer
Darius Chadwick felt his chest tighten with desire as Cygnet Melton glided into his life. But a prelude was all they knew before Cyg fled in despair, certain she had shattered the dream they had made together. Their hearts had collided in an instant; now could they seize the joy of enduring love?

#16 A VERY RELUCTANT KNIGHT
By Billie Green
A tornado brought them together in a storm cel-

lar. But Maggie Sims and Mark Wilding were anything but perfectly matched. Maggie wanted to prove he was wrong about her. She knew they didn't belong together, but when he caressed her, she was swept up in a passion that promised a lifetime of love.

#17 TEMPEST AT SEA
By Iris Johansen
Jane Smith sneaked aboard playboy-director Jake Dominic's yacht on a dare. The muscled arms that captured her were inescapable—and suddenly Jane found herself agreeing to a month-long cruise of the Caribbean. Jane had never given much thought to love, but under Jake's tutelage she discovered its magic . . . and its torment.

#18 AUTUMN FLAMES
By Sara Orwig
Lily Dunbar had ventured too far into the wilderness of Reece Wakefield's vast Chilean ranch; now an oncoming storm thrust her into his arms . . . and he refused to let her go. Could he lure her, step by seductive step, away from the life she had forged for herself, to find her real home in his arms?

#19 PFARR LAKE AFFAIR
By Joan J. Domning
Leslie Pfarr hadn't been back at her father's resort for an hour before she was pitched into the lake by Eric Nordstrom! The brash teenager who'd made her childhood a constant torment had grown into a handsome man. But when he began persuading her to fall in love, Leslie wondered if she was courting disaster.

#20 HEART ON A STRING
By Carla Neggers
One look at heart surgeon Paul Houghton Welling told JoAnna Radcliff he belonged in the stuffy society world she'd escaped for a cottage in Pigeon Cove. She firmly believed she'd never fit into his life, but he set out to show her she was wrong. She was the puppet master, but he knew how to keep her heart on a string.

 # LOVESWEPT

Love Stories you'll never forget by authors you'll always remember

☐	21603	**Heaven's Price #1** Sandra Brown	$1.95
☐	21604	**Surrender #2** Helen Mittermeyer	$1.95
☐	21600	**The Joining Stone #3** Noelle Berry McCue	$1.95
☐	21601	**Silver Miracles #4** Fayrene Preston	$1.95
☐	21605	**Matching Wits #5** Carla Neggers	$1.95
☐	21606	**A Love for All Time #6** Dorothy Garlock	$1.95
☐	21607	**A Tryst With Mr. Lincoln? #7** Billie Green	$1.95
☐	21602	**Temptation's Sting #8** Helen Conrad	$1.95
☐	21608	**December 32nd . . . And Always #9** Marie Michael	$1.95
☐	21609	**Hard Drivin' Man #10** Nancy Carlson	$1.95
☐	21610	**Beloved Intruder #11** Noelle Berry McCue	$1.95
☐	21611	**Hunter's Payne #12** Joan J. Domning	$1.95
☐	21618	**Tiger Lady #13** Joan Domning	$1.95
☐	21613	**Stormy Vows #14** Iris Johansen	$1.95
☐	21614	**Brief Delight #15** Helen Mittermeyer	$1.95
☐	21616	**A Very Reluctant Knight #16** Billie Green	$1.95
☐	21617	**Tempest at Sea #17** Iris Johansen	$1.95
☐	21619	**Autumn Flames #18** Sara Orwig	$1.95
☐	21620	**Pfarr Lake Affair #19** Joan Domning	$1.95
☐	21621	**Heart on a String #20** Carla Neggars	$1.95
☐	21622	**The Seduction of Jason #21** Fayrene Preston	$1.95
☐	21623	**Breakfast In Bed #22** Sandra Brown	$1.95
☐	21624	**Taking Savannah #23** Becky Combs	$1.95
☐	21625	**The Reluctant Lark #24** Iris Johansen	$1.95

Prices and availability subject to change without notice.

Buy them at your local bookstore or use this handy coupon for ordering:

Bantam Books, Inc., Dept. SW, 414 East Golf Road, Des Plaines, Ill. 60016

Please send me the books I have checked above. I am enclosing $_____ (please add $1.25 to cover postage and handling). Send check or money order—no cash or C.O.D.'s please.

Mr/Ms_____

Address_____

City/State_____ Zip_____

SW—9/84

Please allow four to six weeks for delivery. This offer expires 3/85.

LOVESWEPT

*Love Stories you'll never forget
by authors you'll always remember*